THE DINER CON

L. JOSEPH SHOSTY

The Diner Con

THE HARDWOOD CASE FILES

L. Joseph Shosty

For Dad. This series is possible only because of you.

Chapter One

    Herbie's Diner was forty miles south of Sacramento on a stretch of road so lonely the only customers it got in the off-season were dust devils and oak trees. That didn't mean it didn't have its qualities. The honey-battered chicken wasn't bad, and the coffee, while it tasted like it had been strained through a dishrag, did its job of keeping me alert. I probably should not have eaten as much as I had. My powder-blue Chevy was parked at the edge of the lot in case I needed a quick getaway, but I doubted I would be going anywhere quickly, except the john.

    Herbie's was a cramped joint consisting of a twenty-foot counter with nine stools affixed to the concrete floor with heavy steel bolts. The vinyl seat coverings were red, as was the countertop, a glossy enamel. Roughly six feet separated the counter from a row of booths that ran the length of the joint, each giving a view out of plate glass windows. Six feet might sound like a lot of space, but when you have a packed house, that's barely enough room for two people to pass one another without someone having to turn sideways to squeeze by. Behind the counter was the kitchen, partitioned off and unknowable from where I sat, though I'd worked a grill a time or two in the past and could likely draw a map of it without having set foot inside.

At the far end of the room was a swinging door with a small, diamond-shaped window inset at eye level. Beyond the door was the aforementioned john, and next to it was a pay phone. I watched Mort Peters through the window as he spoke into the receiver. He did more talking than listening, which told me plenty about who was on the other end. Occasionally he would stop, listen, then nod, and afterward start up again. He gestured as he made each point, the way someone who is reassuring another might. After a few minutes he hung up the phone and returned to his seat at the counter.

I sat in the booth closest to the door—again, in case I needed to make a quick exit. It afforded me a clear view of the diner. The only thing I couldn't see clearly was the front door, which was just over my right shoulder, but I didn't expect any trouble from that direction. I had my eye on Mort. He was the guy who had me prowling all over northern California, all the way to the Oregon state line and back again.

To know Mort Peters on paper was to expect a man like Peter Lorre: sly, smelling of cigarettes and clove oil, with a voice like a talking weasel, the kind of guy who would put a knife in your back then eat a sandwich in your kitchen afterward, explaining to your widow why killing you had been your fault, not his. To see him in the flesh was another matter. If not a Peter Lorre, I was at least expecting a man with sweaty armpits and a disheveled tie, eyes darting to and fro, and too much hair tonic holding together a coif that hadn't been washed in days.

Instead, he was a very well put-together gee. He stood about six feet, with the build of a college quarterback. His neat gray suit had been recently pressed, and a dame could fix her hair in the mirror shine of his black shoes. When he wasn't on the phone he had the air of someone who was not concerned about much. He read a two-day-old newspaper with casual interest, and he drank hot tea, not coffee. When he spoke to the day waitress, it was evident that he'd had voice training of some sort. Even if he'd never done professional work, at some point Mort Peters had fancied himself an actor.

The waitress came by with a pot of black coffee. She was a smallish woman, about forty, still had some of her looks left, but she had a hardness to her face. Money and bad men were the only things that left that much stone in a woman. I nudged my cup in her direction, and she served her purpose in life.

"You all set, honey?" she asked me.

"Yeah. Tell your cook to lay off the salt the

next time he fries up a chicken."

She nodded toward the door with the diamond window. "Head's in there if you need it."

"I'll live. What's a guy do for kicks around here?"

"Drive into Sacramento. It ain't exactly Kicks Central Station up there, but it's better than watching paint dry around here."

"No motels, no gin joints?"

She made a face. "Sure. Just turn left at the nearest tree."

"But people live around here."

"Sure. Some. Me. Muncey. He's the guy who salted your bird."

"How about Herbie?"

"Herbie retired. He lives in Reseda with his daughter and her husband. Look, what's this all about? You buying property or something?"

"Maybe. Could be I'm gonna be around for a while. A guy likes to know his prospects."

"Honey, I hate to break it to you, but if you're looking to live in this neck of the woods, your prospects ain't none too good."

I stole the name from the tag she wore over her left breast. "Arlene, don't I know it."

She smiled. "Hey, you ain't from around here, but I could swear I know you from someplace."

"Been to L.A. in the last year or three?"

Arlene thought about it a second, then snapped her fingers. "You're on that billboard!"

she said.

Mort Peters looked up, and I stifled an urge to bolt. We made eye contact, and I smiled at him while replying to her, "Guilty as charged."

"Hardwood, Smoller, and Tate. You're one of those fancy detectives to the stars, right?"

Mort turned back to his tea, a bit too stiffly for my pleasure. Now he was eavesdropping, and you could see the tension building in his shoulders. His move wasn't clear to him yet, but he was working it out. When he made his—if he made his—I had to be just as quick, if not quicker, with mine. Problem was, Muncey's fried chicken was working me something fierce. If I went to relieve myself, Mort Peters would be gone when I got back, and all the luck I'd had thus far in tracking him down would be wasted. That meant I had to do something to take the fire from under his feet.

I shook my head. "No, I'm the guy on the billboard. I'm an actor they hired. Bill Crisp."

"You're not a detective." Arlene's tone said she liked me as a detective far more than she would as an actor. That, ultimately, had been my problem.

"Hate to burst your bubble."

"Don't make any sense to me. You look like a detective."

"That's why they hired me. I played a shamus on Inner Sanctum once or twice."

"Inner Sanctum was a radio show. Nobody could see you on the radio."

"Turns out I sound like one, too."

"I don't think we ever had anyone famous in here before."

"You still haven't."

Mort Peter's shoulders shook a little. My wisecrack did more for oiling his gears than it did in sending Arlene packing. Now she was really into her miniature Inquisition.

"So what're you doing up this way? You're a long way from L.A."

"Sacramento has a nice little repertory company. I'm thinking of doing some summer stock. L.A.'s too much of a cesspool. I need a stage to air my grievances."

Arlene shook her head. "Wouldn't know anything about any of that. I keep to myself out here."

That shook her loose, and she went into the back, hopefully to beat a little sense into Muncey for fixing such a wonderful bird only to salt it like it was going to be mummified later.

Mort Peters went back to his newspaper. I tried to gauge his state of mind by staring at the back of his head, but I got nothing of any use. My stomach gurgled, and I patted myself down for an effervescent, to no avail. My hand did fall onto a pack of Luckys, though, and I substituted one of them as a cure for what ailed me.

The sound of my lighter flipping shut roused Peters from his paper. He turned his head to look at me. "May I trouble you for a light?" he asked.

I held out my Zippo. "It's all yours."

Peters came to my table and produced a Charleston from a crinkled pack. This surprised me. With his natty dress, I'd half expected a cigarette case.

"Thanks," he said, and blew smoke from the side of his mouth. "I couldn't help overhearing your conversation with our waitress. You're an actor?"

"Something of one, yeah."

"I did a little acting myself, once. When I lived in New York, that is. But that was years ago." He held out a manicured hand. "Wyatt Link," he said. I took the hand and responded in kind.

This forced me into a role I wasn't comfortable playing. To play the part he was expecting, I had to pretend interest. I made a gesture at the seat across from me. He thanked me and slid in. "Are you from New York?" I asked.

"Nobody is from New York," he drawled. "Only a bunch of Italians and Jews. No, I'm from Vermont, originally. Did a little rep work there before I moved to The Big Apple. Wonderful place. Have you ever been?"

"No," I lied. "I've lived on the West Coast my entire life."

He nodded. "There are worse places to be from," he said. "Now, I haven't been to L.A. in some time, but I recognize your face, too. None of this billboard business, either. Where have I seen you?" I moved to protest, but he held up a hand to stop me. "Oh, come on, now. No need to be modest. It was that one with Joe Cotten in it, wasn't it?"

"Never worked with him."

"No?"

"Did a few Bob Steele westerns. I tend to get shot in the first reel."

Peters nodded. "I don't watch westerns, I'm afraid."

"Good stuff. The good guy always wins."

"Everyone is a good guy in his own mind," Peters said.

"Yeah, but it's society who has the ultimate say. Wouldn't you agree?"

He looked away and took a drag from his cigarette. "Society doesn't have all the facts," he said finally. "Who are they to judge?"

"I'll admit it's a leaky raft, but it's the best idea that's come along yet. Find a better way to keep the human race going, and I'll sign the petition. Until then, justice is justice."

He smiled at me. It was the kind of smile that got beat up by the tougher smiles in grade school.

"I have friends who would agree with you, but I'm not so sure anymore." He crushed out the remains of his cigarette and slid out of the seat. "Well, anyway. Thanks for the light."

"Don't mention it."

He went back to his stool and resumed

reading his newspaper. I wanted to kick myself in the teeth. Not smart, kid, not smart at all. I had just about spilled the beans to him right there with my brash talk of justice. If he was fishing, he'd just landed the twenty-five pounder. Unless he was a first-class rube, which I knew from his file he most certainly was not, then Peters was onto me. I kept both eyes on him after that.

Arlene came out of the back with a fresh pot of coffee and headed straight for my table. Her mouth was a hard line. Had she had words with Muncey, or had I said something to offend? She'd taken off like a shot when I'd mentioned theatre work. I wondered if that had something to do with it. She filled my cup, and I thanked her.

Mort Peters stood up, and I nearly did a spit take. At first, I thought he would throw in and leave. Instead, he pushed through the swinging door, but he didn't stop at the pay phone the way I expected. He went into the john and pulled the door closed behind him.

"How much do I owe you?" I asked Arlene, but I was already sliding out of my seat.

"You don't wanna stick around? I got an apple pie cooling."

"I don't know." I looked around. "Maybe."

"You should. I make the best pie in the state."

"Lemme settle up, and then I'll think about it."

I tossed a few bills onto the counter and told her to keep the change. She said nothing about her tip.

"Why don't you go check on that pie, and I'm gonna run to my car for a bit. If I'm having a slice, I may as well grab a script I've been looking at. You can never know your lines too well, you know."

She nodded and did as she was told, and I practically kicked the glass door open getting outside. Two cars were in the parking lot other than mine, a broken down Ford and a brand-new blue Pontiac. Unless Arlene or Muncey had come into a recent windfall, I could only assume the Pontiac belonged to Peters. His file said he drove a Chrysler, but he could have switched.

I crouched behind the car and went into my left hip pocket. Right side for the brass knucks, left side for the switch knife. You could never be too safe, was my theory. I popped the blade and shoved it into the sidewall. The tire hissed and began to deflate. The knife went back into my pocket, and I was back inside the diner before anyone knew I was gone. If Mort Peters made his move now, he'd be doing it on foot or taking a good twenty minutes to change the tire. Either way, I'd just created some breathing room for myself, which was good, considering the chicken was not to be denied.

I sat down and lit another cigarette, smoked the hell out of it so it would look like

I'd been at it for a bit, and then had some coffee. My body relaxed, despite my queasy stomach. A sense of satisfaction warmed my chest.

Arlene came out of the back, and just as the swinging door closed, I caught a glimpse of Muncey watching me from inside the kitchen. He was a big guy, arms like a body builder, with a head that was clean and shiny. He stared straight at me as the door swung closed, like he was looking for me. I sipped at my coffee. Whatever I'd said to rile Arlene had riled Muncey, as well. I smiled at him, still playing the fool. He wasn't impressed. The door stopped flapping, and that was the last of him.

"More coffee?" Arlene asked.

"Thanks."

She filled my cup. I hoped she didn't notice the sheen of sweat on my forehead, or the breathing I was fighting to get under control. She made no mention of either, and I put my eyes back onto the doorway where I'd last seen Peters. He still wasn't back from the john. Either he was having the same distress I was, or he was making his move. The Pontiac was not visible from where I sat, and I'd have to crane my neck to see it. I hoped it wouldn't come to that. I didn't want to be too obvious.

"You know who makes a good detective, is that Humphrey Bogart," Arlene said. "He looks like a guy who peeks through windows and such."

"The sun does a pretty good job of keeping

15

the Earth warm, too."

Arlene crossed her arms and gave me an arch look. "You're a fresh young man, you know that? Muncey's none too happy with your assessment of his bird, neither. Ever see The Big Sleep?"

"Of course. And The Maltese Falcon."

"Ever play a detective in a movie?"

"No. Just on the radio."

Her face pinched harder than before. My answers were not suiting her at all. "I just don't understand why nobody would cast you as a detective," she said. "You know who's a good one?"

I tried not to roll my eyes. "Basil Rathbone?"

"Who's that?"

"Sherlock Holmes."

"Oh, I don't watch those limey movies. I can't understand their accents. Boston Blackie. What's his real name?"

"Chester Morris."

"He's a good one."

"I wouldn't say he looks like a detective."

"Sure, he does."

"Well, if you mean the kind of guy who wears a suit and occasionally does detective work, I'd have to disagree. Boston Blackie is more of a thug who beats up the right guys."

"Ever been in a fistfight?"

"A few. And I've lost most of them."

"Well, you're an actor." She made the word

16

sound like it had syphilis and a crippled leg.

"How about that pie?"

"It's coming. Think the other guy might want some?"

"I couldn't tell you. Maybe you should go ask him."

"Nah. He'll be in there a while."

"Why do you think that?"

Of all the movies I've seen, none strike me so acutely as the ones where the good guy doesn't realize the fix is in until just the moment when the bad guy is ready to strike. His indication always seems to be from something external, too. For me, it was the loud crash from the john. Mort Peters chose that very moment to fall unconscious and hit the floor. Arlene gave me a flat smile.

"Call it a hunch," she said. "You're right. You ain't much of a detective, after all, but you're done lying to me, hear? When we're through with you, you're gonna tell me everything."

"Arlene, what are you talking about?" And just then, the first wave of dizziness hit. Just like that, I knew she had me. Any second Muncey would come out of the back, bringing something significant with him: a bag, a rope, a gun. That's how it happened in the movies. My eyes clouded up, and Arlene started to get fuzzy. I tried my arm, and it moved, but it felt like it had lead weights attached.

I turned sideways in the booth and leaned

back against the wall, took out a cigarette, and struggled with lighting it.

"Not putting up much of a struggle, eh?"

"What's the point? Mickey Finn is gonna have his way with me regardless of what I do."

"You're right about that."

"Am I going to wake up?"

Arlene laughed a little. "You'll just have to wait and see. You gonna finish the rest of that cigarette?"

I'd pulled the cigarette from my lips what felt like only a second ago, but looking down at it I saw that it had burnt down to the halfway point. How long had I been sitting there?

"No," I said. "It doesn't look like I am. You want it?"

"Maybe. Been on my feet twelve hours already."

"Your relief coming soon?"

"You wish."

That was the last thing I remembered.

Chapter Two

I woke sometime later. At first, I thought I'd come to in an athlete's dirty sock bin, only it turned out to be the bandana tied across my eyes had seen some use and hadn't been washed before becoming my blindfold. I was tied to something cool and hard and round and broad enough that my hands didn't touch when they were tied behind me. It could have been a column of some sort, but it was more than likely a tree. I felt a breeze, but that could have been anything. Everything around me was deathly silent.

My mouth was dry, and I wished I had a cigarette. I coughed some the way I did when I woke in the morning. Coffee would be nice, too. My stomach growled. None of the previous discomfort remained. I wondered what had happened in that regard.

"You awake?"

Arlene.

"If this is a dream, I'm firing my agent."

"Still cracking wise, huh? Well, we'll see about that."

"Is Muncey gonna come 'round and give me the business? That's a pretty funny thing to do after you've gone to all the trouble to tie me up in the middle of nowhere."

"It ain't the middle of nowhere, but it's close. And yeah, Muncey will see to your wise-cracking face soon enough. You won't like what he does with it once he has it, though."

"Tell him to stay away from the eyes but have fun with the rest. I've always wanted to do horror. Universal can save on makeup if Muncey does a real number on me."

This actually elicited a chuckle from her. She was moving around me, doing something that I couldn't see or hear. It sounded like she was flicking a lighter over and over again. Was she lighting candles around me, or torches? She could have been starting a forest fire, for all I knew.

"So what is all this about, Arlene? Do you make it a habit of kidnapping people and killing them in the forest where no one can see you do it?"

"Not everyone. Just liars like you."

"Like me? What have I lied about?"

"You know you're a detective. All that about you being an actor is bunk. I seen you on that billboard."

"And I told you the truth about that. I was hired to pose for that photo."

"Bunk."

"It's the truth."

"Bunk!"

I sighed.

"Believe what you want. I can't stop you."

"Then why were you in the diner today? And don't give me any of that about you going up to Sacramento to do theatre stuff. Muncey and I worked in the theatre for years. The Carlisle up there went belly up a year ago. And there ain't another house to be had. Unless you go up there in a time machine, your story was bunk. No two ways about it."

"You were in the theatre? What'd you do?"

"Make up. Muncey did lighting."

"Where'd you work?"

"None of your business, that's where."

"Did we do a show together, maybe?"

"I wouldn't know. I had a hundred pretty boys like you in my chair at one time or another. You're a face in the crowd, mister."

"I was dashing enough you remembered me from the billboard."

Arlene chuckled again. She was standing in front of me now. I heard her light up and pull from a cigarette. My mouth started to water for the taste of one. My fingers twitched to hold it to my lips.

"Listen, I think you have the wrong idea about me. Truth time, all right? All on the table. I can guess you're in trouble. You were in the theatre. Swell. But something must have happened so you aren't anymore. I can hear it in your voice. You want to go back, don't you? I don't know what you did, Arlene, and I don't care. I'm a private eye. You're right. But I never lied to you. I'm also an actor. Only, when I took that job for Hardwood, Smoller, and Tate I got a reputation. I don't know how, or why. Who can know? Only, when I'd show up to read for a part I'd get the aren't-you-that-guy questions, and no one would hire me. Later I found out that Hardwood, Smoller, and Tate was a front for a high-end smash and grab operation. I was out of work a while. Nearly destitute. So I decided if people could only believe I was a detective, I'd become one. I got my license. I even took the name Johnny Hardwood so people would believe I was the real thing. And yeah, I'm on a case right now, but it has nothing to do with you."

There was a long silence. I could hear Arlene smoking, could feel the stillness of her standing there, lax posture, sizing me up with her eyes and ears. After a while she asked, "So why were you there?"

"The other guy in the diner. His name is Mort Peters. I don't know how you can check that out, but that's his name. He goes by a number of aliases, including Wyatt Link, but his name is Mort Peters. He was a big shot at All-American Studios for a while, a behind-the-scenes kind of guy who handled funding for pictures."

"A producer."

"Yeah. A producer. A few months ago, he absconded with some money. A few million. He hid it all over the place. Ten thousand here, twenty there. Then he pulled a disappearing act, too. Cops found his wife's Bentley in a lake. There was a body in it, only the fish had gotten to it so bad an ID couldn't be made. I was put on the case to make certain he was dead and not pulling a fast one. I discovered an insurance policy with his wife as benefactor, only by then she was living hand-to-mouth in a flophouse back East in Red Hook. Someone impersonated her in California and got the payout, then disappeared just like Peters. This made me think our guy wasn't dead after all but working with people to make a little retirement money. Through a series of lucky breaks, I found a cousin in Sacramento. I was up there to check it out when, two days ago, who did I see walking out of a laundry service? I've tailed him ever since. Followed him here because I figured he was picking an out-of-the-way place to contact whoever is working with him. He made several phone calls from your joint; you must have seen that."

"The guy's loaded?"

"Like Fort Knox."

There was another pause. Finally, Arlene said, "Wait here."

"I'll try, but I've got a business meeting at four."

She said nothing to the wisecrack, and I heard her walk off, crunching leaves underfoot.

I ran down my situation. First, I tested my bonds. The rope was thick, like the kind you'd see mooring a boat to a dock. Or the kind used in the theatre to suspend curtains and the like, the kind that didn't break or fray because lives depended on it holding together. I wasn't bound tightly. My arms ached, but I'd live. No injuries to my body, either. At least Muncey hadn't gotten squirrely with me after I'd passed out. That told me plenty. These two were in control of themselves. I wondered what they had done to score themselves so much heat. Theft? Murder? Either one would have had the police jumping like salmon.

I wriggled my hips to feel for that tell-tale lump in my pants. It wasn't there. So they had my wallet. It had my ID, my fake ID with the Johnny Hardwood alias, and my detective's license. It also had my SAG card as well as a small booklet full of names and numbers of agents, all of whom had neglected to return my calls after the offers had started to dry up. That meant they knew what I'd told them about my identity was square. If they'd bothered to go through my jacket pocket they'd find the photo I had of Peters. If they hadn't they probably wouldn't believe me. Of course, none of that mattered now. They'd tipped their hand to me, and they couldn't allow me to leave, not on the off-chance I'd rat them out to the authorities. I needed an angle.

I was in the middle of not knowing what that angle would be when I heard the shouting. I couldn't tell how far away it was, but I could recognize Arlene's raw, gravelly voice and another, a man's, which I could only take for Muncey. Certainly the voice was higher pitched than I'd have imagined it, given Muncey's size, but I don't judge. A big guy didn't mean he had a low, rough voice any more than being fat meant a guy was a glutton.

Arlene's voice became louder and more pronounced, which said she was moving closer to me and arguing with Muncey at the same time.

"—for, ya bum," were the first words I

could make out clearly. Trouble in paradise.

"Something the matter?" I asked.

"Don't you never mind," Arlene said. "I swear, you men don't have the brains God gave a pig."

The moment wasn't right for me to tell her pigs were intelligent, I could feel it. "I couldn't help but overhear you arguing with Muncey."

"Really? What'd you hear?"

"Not much, just angry voices. Something I can help with?"

"Oh, I'll bet you could help us out real good, couldn't you?" she sneered. "Well, your story checks out, at least about being an actor and a detective, but I guess you know that."

"Yeah. I had a feeling it would. You can keep the twenty bucks, by the way."

"Y'know, you're gonna get it a lot easier around here if you ixnay on the wisecracks, Hardwood."

"Probably, but then that wouldn't be in character, now, would it? Come on, Arlene, tell me what's wrong. If I can help, I will. You have my word on that."

"What can you do?"

"I can't know that until you tell me."

The frustration was plain, and when Arlene spoke, her voice shook, like someone who was gesturing violently. "Ah, who needs it, anyway? I told that man to go easy on your pal. Such a well-put-together guy, you know? Figured him for a banker or something. We could maybe

25

make a little scratch off him. 'Go easy,' I says, but does he listen?"

"Muncey did something to him, Arlene?"

"I'll say."

"What happened?"

The silence was all I needed to know.

"So Peters is dead. That's disheartening."

"Yeah. Doesn't bode well for you, does it? Muncey's gone to dump the body, and I expect we'll tend to you when he gets back."

"Doesn't make sense to dump the bodies one at a time. Why not call him back?"

"You're an awful easy customer for somebody who's staring down his maker."

"Because I know something that might make killing me a boneheaded move."

"What's that?"

"Get Muncey back here before he takes off and does something stupid, and we'll talk. I want both of you to hear it."

"He's probably already left."

"A couple million dollars might light a fire under you to find out."

"What?"

"You heard me. Go."

The bluff worked. Arlene took off like a shot. Her gone gave me the breathing room I needed, but it wouldn't last long. I had to work fast. Think, Hardwood. This was the moment in the movie where the detective always pulls something clever out of his hat. Only, this wasn't the movies. This was real. The worst

kind of real. Muncey was apparently a casual
gee when it came to violence, and Arlene was
complicit in his crimes, maybe even the brains
behind the brawn. They would make a corpse
out of me just as fast as Muncey had done for
Mort Peters. Maybe quicker. There was the
wisecrack about Muncey's chicken, after all,
and some guys have no sense of humor. Arlene
certainly didn't, and that was not playing in my
favor. All we had in common was that we didn't
like the current situation, and that we all
wanted some kind of payoff for the day going to
Hell. That gave me a hole card, at least.

Arlene returned with Muncey in tow. I
could hear his breathing. Big guys tend to put
out a lot of wind, but he was otherwise keeping
to himself.

"Okay, we're here," Arlene said. "What did
you want to say?"

"I think I can get you Peters' money. Some
of it, anyway."

"How's that?" she asked.

"He's been talking to someone on the
phone all day. I think it's the fake Mrs. Peters
who got the life insurance payout. She's
probably some girl he had on the hook and
thought maybe he would make her a
permanent thing when he ditched the real Mrs.
Peters and took off with All-American's loot.
Five'll get you ten she knows where at least
some of the money can be found."

"How much?"

"I can't tell you that. But it has to be enough to keep her happy. I don't know the fake Mrs. Peters, but I know the type. If she can't have her man, she'll need some kind of distraction: shopping, pedicures, new hairdos. Women like to pamper themselves when there isn't someone along to do it for them."

Arlene snorted.

"Present company excluded, I suppose."

"So how do we get that money?" she asked.

I shook my head. "That's for me to know and for you to figure out."

"You got a lotta nerve, Hardwood. What's to stop us from putting two in you right now?"

"Do that, and you have two dead bodies and only a twenty and some change to show for it. Sounds like lousy pay for a day's work to me."

"You got a lotta nerve!"

"Don't be thick, Arlene. You two have gotten this far by playing it smart. Don't louse it up now. You gotta know I'm looking to get out of this alive. Knowing the particulars of this caper keeps me that way. If I were to tell you everything now, what's to stop you from sending me to join Peters in some shallow grave?"

Muncey chuckled.

"Okay. So we have to trust each other for a while," Arlene said. "What do we do?"

"You start by taking off this blindfold."

Muncey did so. The first thing I saw was

his big face glaring at me. This, of course, was his intent, to let me know there was to be no funny stuff while he was on watch. I had no intentions of taking any chances until I had a better idea of my circumstances.

Evening had set in. We were in a clearing in the midst of an old-growth forest. The world was suddenly very close and suffocating. The sounds I had heard earlier of Arlene playing with my cigarette lighter had been her lighting a number of tiki torches that she had set up around the edges of the clearing. The ground was well-trampled, and a number of cast-off items lay around me. Apparently I was not the first person brought to this spot.

It made me wonder how long this had been occurring, and if I was smart in playing games with a couple of psychopaths. Not that I had a choice. It took little deduction to see that they had intended—and probably still intended—to kill me.

Muncey produced a large hunting knife and sawed through my bonds. The ropes fell away, and I rubbed my wrists, not because they were sore, but more as an automatic reaction. Muncey returned to stand next to Arlene. They had changed out of their diner uniforms and were dressed more like lumberjacks in flannel shirts, denim jeans, and sturdy workbooks. Arlene had her hair tied back with a shoelace. She, too, had a knife. Muncey's knuckles, I noticed, were scraped and bloodied, presumably from the working over he had given Peters. If I had to choose a way to go, being beaten to death by a gorilla was not high on the list.

"What time is it?" I asked.

"A little after six."

"Okay, we need to get back to the diner."

"Why?"

"I need to make a phone call or two."

"To who?"

"My stockbroker."

Arlene looked at Muncey. "You see what I'm talking about? Can you imagine me letting some two-bit pretty boy like him get so fresh with me?"

Muncey smiled to placate her. As far as he was concerned, they weren't going to suffer me much longer, at any rate.

Chapter Three

Arlene extinguished the torches, and we walked in near-total darkness for what seemed like a hundred miles but was probably no more than a hundred yards. The trees broke in a brief respite that was probably a trail or lane. The broken-down Ford was parked nearby. They led me to the car. Arlene got in behind the wheel, and Muncey gestured for me to sit in the front seat. He slid into the back seat directly behind me. Arlene started the car and backed it slow and easy down the lane until we hit the main road. She turned south, and we started driving.

"Just curious," I said, "but where have you got Peters?"

"The trunk," Arlene said. "Why?"

"Just wanting to know where all the players are."

"How do you figure Peters being a player?" Arlene asked.

"He's got a big part in this. Like for instance, if you get stopped by a cop, you should know I'm going to start singing like a canary."

"And you should know if a cop pulls us over, I'm gonna put a knife through the back of your skull and take my chances," Muncey said in his too-high voice.

"See? Everyone is a player here, even Muncey."

"What's that supposed to mean?" Muncey asked.

"Nothing. Let's drive."

Arlene did as told. The speedometer read a steady thirty-five miles per on the way back. It took roughly twelve to fifteen minutes before we reached Herbie's Diner. I filed that information away in case I needed it, though it was more likely that I would never find the clearing where they had kept me, even if I searched. I wasn't sure that I would ever need to, but I liked to know as much as I could about an op. It tended to boost my confidence, which came in handy when things looked grim.

The diner was dark, and a sign in the window said it was closed for repairs. Arlene unlocked the door and went inside. She turned on a few lights, but nothing more than was needed. She left the sign in the window to discourage customers. Muncey nudged me inside.

Arlene was on automatic pilot. She started brewing the coffee before she even knew what she was doing but recovered by asking Muncey if he wanted any. He grunted. I bummed a cigarette off him and mentioned I wouldn't mind a cup. My captors looked at me like I owed them money. I went to make my phone call.

Muncey made to follow me, but I stopped by the swinging door. "Look, I do this alone, or you can just put two in my head right now."

He grinned at me. "Maybe I'll do that."

"This is going to be difficult enough without you breathing down the back of my neck, Muncey. I need to have my wits about me."

He gave me the eye. "Fine, but I'll be right outside the door. Try any funny stuff, like calling the cops, and I'll know it."

I pushed through into the little hallway. At the far end was the john. I thought of how Mort

Peters had gone there after being drugged, probably to splash some water on his face from the basin, all the while thinking it was the strain of his situation making him ill, never realizing Arlene and Muncey had his number.

I thought about what Peters' last moments must have been like. He'd probably been tied to a tree, just like me. It made no sense. Why let a gorilla like Muncey pound on him? He was a producer, a salesman, the kind used to proposing nebulous, iffy deals. Why hadn't he offered Muncey some of the money? It made no sense to me. The ideal would have been to ask him, but that was impossible now.

I picked up the receiver and dialed. An operator with a husky, sexy voice picked up. "How may I connect you?" she asked.

"Look, I made several calls from this line earlier today, but I lost the number. Could you be a dear and look it up for me?"

"One moment." She came back with a number, Malibu-69755. I nearly choked. The number was in West Hollywood. Half a state away. It could have been worse, of course. It could have been New York, or the moon, but it was doubtful Arlene or Muncey's mood was going to improve when they learned the truth. I asked the operator to connect me and filed the number away in case I needed it later.

"Collect call to that number, then, from Mort."

"One moment while I direct, sir."

A pouty, dimwitted voice answered. "Mort? Darling, what's the matter? I thought you said we weren't supposed to talk after six."

"Mrs. Peters, I presume?" I said.

There was a long pause. I imagined blonde pincurls beneath a pretty, if vacuous, face doing its best deer-in-the-headlights impression. The receiver was slightly away from her face, and she was torn between answering and hiding in the closet. I couldn't let her get away; she might never answer her phone again.

"Don't hang up, Mrs. Peters. Mort's life depends on you cooperating. Do you understand?"

A little girl version of the voice came back over the line. "Is he okay?"

"For now. Whether or not he stays that way is entirely up to you. I say this not to scare you, but to impress upon you the gravity of this situation."

"May I speak to him?"

"No, you may not. You can talk to him all you want later, when we have what we want. Until then, you talk to me. I'm your best friend for the next few days. And ma'am, I don't want anything to happen to him, either. I want everything to go smoothly, and then we'll all go our separate ways, but that only happens if you play ball. Do you understand?"

"Yes. What do you want?"

"The money, naturally."

"What money?"

I turned on the menace. "Now, see, that's
not very smart of you. It's just that kind of
funny business that's going to wind up with
some postal employee finding a body in a ditch.
Capisce?"

Mrs. Peters issued a squeak of terror. "I'm
sorry, I'm sorry!" she cried.

I felt a knot working into my gut. She was
really afraid. Whatever kind of man Mort
Peters might have been, and whatever kind of
girl this young lady might be, it did not take a
swami to see that she loved him. If I had been
more of a man I would have found another way
out of this, but right then I was playing to get
out alive. I don't know what that said about me,
but I would have worked the same play on my
mother if it had a chance of getting me away
from Muncey and Arlene.

"That's better. Any more of that, and I hang
up. And Mrs. Peters, if I hang up, I won't be
calling back. It's up to you to keep me on this
phone, so you had better play it straight from
here on out."

"I will. Just don't hurt Mort. He hasn't
done anything."

"Sure, he has. He's done plenty. That's how
you're sitting on a pile of dough."

"How do you know that?"

"He told me."

"He did?"

"Yeah."

"Cuz he told me people might be calling, trying to trick me into telling them stuff. He said not to talk to anyone."

"I'm not with those people. I'm with me."

"How do I know that?"

"Because I know that Mort has been in Sacramento, and that his cousin, Paul, has been doing his dry cleaning for him. I know that he's fond of a gray suit with a powder blue tie that doesn't go with it, that he probably wears because you bought it for him, and I know he's been calling you collect from Herbie's Diner south of Sacramento periodically all day. Now if I know that much about him, the question you have to ask is, if I was with the people who want their money back, why wouldn't I just beat its location out of him and go get it?"

There was another long pause while she processed the information. "So why don't you beat the location out of him anyways? Why call me at all?"

Not bad. My opinion of the faux Mrs. Peters improved.

"Because I'm a businessman, Mrs. Peters. I found out what I did with coercion, not muscle. I don't want to be that man, but if you don't cooperate, I'll be forced to cut my losses and move on. That means doing a lot more than just beating a guy like Mort for information. I'd rather do this easy and get him home safely to you ASAP. Now, listen. I want the money, as much of it as you can scrape together."

There was a pause. "There is no money."

"What did I say about playing games with me? I'm hanging up, Mrs. Peters."

"No! Wait! Please, I'm not trying to trick you. Please believe me. There was money, a lot of it, but there isn't any. Not anymore."

"You spent it?"

"No. Oh, no. Morty thought...well, we talked it over, and we thought it would be a good idea to take what we had and fold it into a business interest."

"What kind of interest?"

"A movie."

It made sense. A guy like Peters was smart, but he was also a gambler. It wasn't the notion of making money that got a guy like him out of bed in the morning. It was in the risk of failing or coming up big. A move like this would satisfy that need, and then some. Further, he could show a Herculean chutzpah and invest his stolen money in the very thing that had made him rich to begin with. I wouldn't be surprised if the money was tied up in All-American Pictures, the same people he had bilked, through some dummy company, as a matter of fact. That would have been the ultimate jab and twist of the knife to the people he'd robbed, to use the money he'd stolen to make a killing on a sure thing, and then disappear forever. Talk about the crime of the century. The sheer scope of the scheme did little for my gut, though. Arlene and Muncey were not going to be happy if they found out.

"You can't have put everything into it. You need money to live on, and you don't strike me as a gal who likes to operate from Skid Row."

This hardened her up a bit. "You don't know a thing about me," she said. "I've been on the bottom. I can make do."

"How much have you been making do with?"

"About forty-thousand."

"You're a real martyr. All right, look. I know Peters would never let his wife handle his affairs while he's away: it's too risky. And anyway, women don't negotiate movie deals. That means there's been a friend of your husband's around to handle the leg work. Am I right?"

"Arthur Hands. His name is Arthur Hands."

"He doesn't need to know about this. Do you understand? He gets nowhere near this, or you never see your husband again. Got it?"

"O-okay."

"Good." I gave her directions to Herbie's Diner and that she had until five tomorrow afternoon to get the money to me. She tried to keep me on the line, but I hung up.

I felt sick.

Muncey and Arlene were waiting for me when I returned to the dining room. The lights were on, but the Closed for Repairs sign was still up in the window. I bummed a cigarette from Arlene's pack.

"So?" she asked.

The first drag made its exit through my nostrils. "So, she fell for it."

"What's the score?"

"Couldn't say. There's a lot of money in this deal, and she doesn't have a head for figures."

"Speculate, then."

I let go of a long plume of smoke. "She's going to hold out on us. That much is a given. Women like her lie so much, it's second nature. But she's going to scrounge enough that I think you're going to be pleased."

"Quit stalling, pretty boy."

"You could see as much as a million."

Chapter Four

They haven't invented the words to describe the looks I got. Until then it had probably seemed like a dream. Maybe it was a last gasp of some guy who was desperate not to end up rotting in an orchard somewhere. Whatever the case, they hadn't considered the scam I was proposing was real. Finally, after a series of twitches and jerks had rolled across their faces, Muncey smiled. It was genuine. It was also more horrifying than his scowl ever was.

"That's something," he said.

"Yep. We're gonna be rich," I replied.

Arlene snorted.

"We? Who's 'we', huh?"

"The three of us."

"And you think you're gonna get some of this, huh? Maybe the best you can hope for is we let you walk away from this with your skin intact. No way you're getting scratch, too. You got way too high an opinion of yourself."

"Oh, I'm getting a little," I said, "and I'll tell you why. If I get part of the money— just a small part, mind you—then I'm complicit in the crime. You can let me go, and there's no way I can squeal without going down with you. Look, if I get back to L.A. I'm getting nothing for all my hard work. Peters is dead, and All-American is never getting their money back. Most of what I stood to make on this case was contingent on returning the money. You guys are going to have that money, not me, so I get nothing. I'm broke to begin with, and my rep is going to take a serious hit. It's going to be six months or more before a warm body even walks through the door, and it'll be another six months before the cases are worth my time again. That's a long time to be living on boiled potatoes and cheap whiskey. I might get desperate, and my mouth might start to squawk a little about a charming greasy spoon outside Sacramento.

"Now, you can kill me. Sure you can. Muncey is twice my size, and I'm unarmed. So, I'm at your mercy. I know that. So I'm not even pretending otherwise. But then you won't have the advantage anymore."

"Who needs an advantage when it's just some broad showing up to deliver the loot?"

"You'll need it because she is a broad, as you put it. What's a woman do better than anything in the world?"

Muncey piped up immediately. "Talk. Boy, do they like it."

"Exactly. Do you think she's not going to tell someone where she's going, and if she's not back in, say, two days, to call the cops?"

"So? What can she tell people?" Arlene asked.

"A lot."

"So the cops look around an empty lot or a patch of field. So what?"

"I told her the drop-off point is here."

Arlene's eyes narrowed.

"Now why would you go and do a thing like that?"

"For my security."

"That's not smart, mister, lemme tell you."

"Maybe not, but that's how it shakes out."

"You need to call her back and arrange for a different drop."

"No."

Arlene was angry, and indeed she should be. I had thrown her plan, which was to kill me,

41

take the money, and probably kill Mrs. Peters as well, into a tizzy. Now everything was messy. People like Arlene didn't handle messy well. As long as they were in control of a situation, they could be formidable. Take them outside their usual territory, and they would get sloppy, start to panic. I had no illusions that they would modify their plan, which still included killing me, but now they had to plan for things that they could not easily control, like the possibility of customers coming by, snooping around for a bowl of chili whether the Open sign was up or not.

Arlene fished another cigarette from her pocket, and with a shaky hand got a light. "You got a lot of nerve," she said. I had definitely misjudged her level of cool. She looked ready to scrap the whole thing and put a bullet in my brain. I had to do something to keep the peace.

"If you were in my place, you'd have done the same thing. Now, look, this is still your show. I just want to keep things on an even keel. You're angry with me for being such a wisenheimer. I get that. You want blood. But you have to look beyond that to something far more profitable than just seeing my head on a stick. There's a lot of money coming your way. I want just enough of a taste to make me a part of the conspiracy. That's insurance for you, not for me, that I don't say anything."

"And what do we do about this chippy who's showing up with the cash?" Arlene said.

"Her hubby's dead in our trunk. You don't think she's gonna be angry when she finds out what we done?"

"Maybe, but once we show her we're wise to her, she'll be too afraid to do anything."

"How are we to do that?"

"By taking out her insurance policy."

"Come again?"

"Arthur Hands."

"I don't think I follow."

"I told you about Mort Peters stealing a lot of money from these movie people, right? Well, I don't know if I told you the rest. It's been a long day, after all. But Peters faked his own death. His widow—his real widow—buried the wrong guy after the cops fished his car out of a lake. Now, a guy like Peters is many things, but he's not a killer. No, he's a powerful man. Or was. When you're powerful, you don't get your hands dirty. You find a man who is capable of doing the nasty things that you need done with little or no remorse. For that, you need an animal. A real monster. For Mort Peters, that guy is Arthur Hands. He'll be coming up here with the wife."

"How do you know this?"

"Because I told her not to bring him."

Arlene shook her head. "That don't make no sense."

"I specifically mentioned Hands in case he wasn't already in her head. By putting him there, we ensure that she calls him. Likely, she'll need him to put together the money, anyway, as I doubt Peters left her in charge of its location. But he'll come, and she'll have the confidence of having a gorilla like him in her corner."

"Only that evens the odds for her side."

"Not exactly. See, we know he's coming, so we have a chance to prepare for him. He'll do nothing overt. In fact, we probably won't see him at all unless the deal goes south, which we know it will. His first priority will be to his boss. He wants Peters back, and he'll play ball until then. If he can make us pay for the inconvenience, he will, but that's not his focus.

"Muncey, you're going to lie in wait for him. He'll have Mrs. Peters drop him somewhere away from the diner. Either that or he'll have her park out of sight so he can slip out of the car. Regardless, you'll be outside to keep an eye on his approach. I imagine he's a pretty tough guy if he's got the drop on you, but he'll be a plate of beans if he can't find the upper hand.

"You deal with him, and you bring me evidence of him that she'll recognize. This way, I can show her that we have the whole thing figured. She'll be near hysterics, but I think I can convince her not to make a scene. She'll toss in the money, and you'll give me a cut off the top. We then tell her that Mort is in Sacramento, and that I'll drive her to his location. I plan to take a long, leisurely route, so the two of you will have ample time to get out of town. Then, I'll drop her at the first bus station I come to, and I'll disappear for a while before making it back to L.A. She's out money, her husband, her husband's bodyguard, and all that, but she's alive. A girl like her is dumb as a bag of hammers, but even she can figure that getting out with her life is a big payout."

The two sat a while, chewing over my plan. I tried to keep a straight face and not betray any of what I was feeling. It wouldn't serve me for them to know that I had just rehashed the plot of a film script I'd read several years ago but had never gone into production.

Arlene already thought little of me. If she could just be convinced a little while longer that I was a useless punk out to save his own skin, this might work. I wasn't worried about Muncey. I could tell by the look in his eyes he liked his part in this. Anything that involved breaking someone's head was all right with him. It was Arlene I had to convince. For better or worse, she was the brains of their operation. If she said it was a go, we were good. Otherwise, I felt like I would be joining Mort in the trunk of the rusted-out Ford pretty soon.

"You got this all figured, don't you?" Arlene said at last. She was on her fourth cigarette since I had returned from making my phone call.

"Do you have a better plan?" I asked.
"Maybe."
"Let's hear it."

"I said 'maybe', and anyway, you aren't calling the shots around here."

"Okay. What do you think?"

"I like the part where we get the money, but I don't like you getting a cut, no matter how small."

"It's like I said—"

"Yeah, I heard what you said. And I don't like the girl getting to live, not after she's seen our faces."

"My face. If we play this right, you're going to run the diner, same as always."

"We got a girl on tomorrow, named Jolene. What do I tell her?"

"Tell her you need to switch shifts with her."

"Okay. I can do that."

"Then you sling coffee, and Muncey handles the kitchen, just like always, until about a half past four. That's when he slips out to handle the Arthur Hands business. What time is your rush?"

Arlene snorted. "We don't never get a rush. We may have some regulars in, though."

"See to them. I'll handle the rest. That way, she'll never know it was you or Muncey who was working with me."

"What about this Hands guy?"

I dragged a thumbnail across my throat. Muncey smiled.

Arlene nodded. "I like that. That means the only person who knows we were even in on it is you."

"Yeah, but don't get any funny ideas about me. After this, I'm going to be a ghost. By the time I show my face to the world again, you two should be somewhere else, preferably Mexico or Canada."

"You ain't worried about the girl fingering you to the cops?"

"To say what, that I stole the money she and her husband stole from a major movie studio? I'm not worried. Chances are, she'll find a nice hole to hide in for about a year until she feels like she can stick her head out again. After that, who cares what she does? Look, as plans go, this one is just about the best for all those concerned. The only hitch is that Peters is dead. If he were alive, it would be perfect. As is, the girl will be upset. Hysterical, even. But she'll get over it. No dame ever really loves so hard that she'll pine the rest of her life away over it. That only happens in the storybooks. Give her three months, and she'll be on some other sucker's elbow, drinking martinis and ordering her cabana boy to bring her more crackers with olive spread."

Arlene grunted. That outlook was just cynical enough for her that she was sold. She poured me a cup of coffee, and we toasted on it. Muncey handed me my cigarettes, minus a holding fee, but I didn't get the Zippo. They weren't trusting me too much, I guess. I smoked and drank my coffee. Muncey asked if I was hungry. I said yes, and he fixed us burgers and hashbrowns on the griddle. I ate with gusto. Muncey watched me eat with an approving look on his face while Arlene made herself scarce for a while.

When I was done Muncey showed me to the little trailer they kept behind the diner. It was a rundown thing that would never have been out of place atop a junk heap, but it kept the rain out, I supposed. There was a tiny bedroom in the back, but that belonged to them. I was given a lime green couch at the front and a ratty blanket to use as a cover.

By then it was about eight o'clock, maybe nine, and I feigned exhaustion and lay down with my face turned inward toward the backrest. I made a good play of pretending sleep, laying stock still for what felt like three hours, but was probably one at most. Arlene came in at some point, and eventually I heard snoring down the hall. I very much wanted another cigarette, but I didn't dare move.

I waited a while longer just for good measure, and then turned over. It was a good thing I had foregone the cigarette, for I would have likely sucked it down my throat in shock when I saw Muncey sitting ten feet away from me in a straight-backed chair, still as a stone, and watching me with very bright, very alert, eyes.

"Don't try any funny stuff," he said.

I put on a muzzy front. "Just getting up to

use the john," I replied. "Don't you ever sleep?"

"I'll sleep when I'm dead," he replied. "Go shake the dew off your lily and get back in here."

I did as told and managed to eke out something from nothing, just to make a show of it. Afterward I went back and curled up on the couch again, but this time I seriously went to sleep. I figured if they wanted me dead, they could make me that way at their leisure. It wouldn't hurt any, then, for me to grab a few hours of shut eye. Tomorrow was my big scene, after all.

I woke again as the gray light of morning was making the room glow in black and white. I rolled over to find Arlene in Muncey's spot, sitting just as still as he had, only the smoke of a recently lit cigarette betraying anything.

"Don't try any funny stuff," she said.

"I'm not," I replied. "Do you and Muncey have the same dialogue coach?"

"You know, I'm just about tired of your funny."

"That's fine. I'm just about tired of your grumpy. At least today we can get all this behind us, eh?"

"Assuming your plan works, or that I don't change it in the meantime."

I found my cigarettes and tucked one between my lips. "What's that supposed to mean?"

"Just what I said."

"Look, Arlene, if you're planning to ruin a perfectly good plan, I wish you'd just take me out back and shoot me right now."

"I can arrange that."

"Then why haven't you?"

She said nothing, instead preferring to smoke another Lucky. The fact she was talking about it told me maybe I was going to see my way out of this alive. If she was staying mum about it, or started giving me claps on the back and attaboys, I would get nervous. It could still go that way, so I kept my eyes sharp for anything that might give her away.

Arlene woke Muncey a little while later, and they went to open the diner. I convinced them of my good intentions and got to stay behind. They let me, but I knew they were watching me, just in case I tried to pull a fast one. I showered first, then brushed my teeth with a strip of toothpaste on my finger. There wasn't much room in the trailer, but I made use of the ironing board so my suit didn't look slept in.

I didn't bother searching for a weapon. By now they surely had removed everything I could use. I did find my Zippo, though, which pleased me.

Chapter Five

I wondered as I arrived at the diner where they had put my piece. I kept my service .45 in a shoulder holster, which they had stripped off me before tying me to the tree yesterday. The question was at what point did they take it? If it was still in the diner, that could come in handy in case everything went south. If it was in their car, I could still make a play for it, though it seemed unlikely I could scrounge a reason to go search. I needed something, anything. The brass knucks would even do the trick, but they were gone, too, along with my knife. I know it's a cliché, but I felt naked.

I walked around the side of the diner rather than go in through the back door. Two new cars were already parked out front. Inside, Arlene was working the counter, pouring coffee for a couple of men dressed like laborers. She watched me as I went to my car, probably realizing for the first time that my plan had created certain conditions that left her all but helpless if I should suddenly decide to walk out and start hitchhiking. On the passenger side seat was a battered dime store historical I'd brought along for the slow stretches in my investigation. I grabbed it off the seat and went inside, taking up the same booth I had occupied the day before. Arlene glared at me as she brought me coffee. I ordered ham and eggs for breakfast; that didn't improve her mood. I figured they could take it out of the twenty they'd copped from my wallet.

There wasn't much left to do but wait and keep a sharp eye out for the next play. I speculated on what that might be for at least an hour before I gave it up. There was no way to divine it out of thin air. I didn't know the faux Mrs. Peters, but I knew desperation. I'd seen some of it when I was in the service. I'd felt it once or twice myself after the war, when I couldn't get work because I'd played one part perhaps too well and no one could see me as anything but. You get a twitchiness of character to match the look in your eyes. Your laugh suddenly becomes a little too wild, and your smile is all teeth. The main thing with desperation is you start to do things a little crazier than usual. You take chances you never would, normally. The most outlandish ideas start to sound credible. If there could be a real story of how I transitioned from playing a detective to being one, it was somewhere within that irrational playground. Luckily for me it had worked out well; it could have just as easily gone in the other direction, ending with me maybe turning to petty crime to keep bread on the table, or worse. I did not like to think about the "or worse" part of it.

The faux Mrs. Peters was feeling desperate right about now. Even with forty grand in the bank, times were lean in the Peters household. Her man was gone, leaving the joint cold and gloomy. Money went to fund two households because he was on the run. There was his right-hand man lurking around all the time, keeping an eye on her that she did not do anything too rash. The real money was tied up with a movie, or perhaps several movies, and there was no telling if or when they would see the payout. And there was the anticipation of knowing that, soon, she might be a very rich woman. That's a lot for one dame to handle.

Now throw me and my hare-brained scheme into the fray. Her little Morty was in the clutches of nefarious street trash, who was holding him in some dirty diner in Darkest Northern California. They wanted all the money, and they were talking with knives and pistols. They were already disappointed to find out there wasn't nearly as much as they thought there should be. The story I'd fed her was that Mort was claiming millions. That told her that Mort was still looking to get out of this alive, and that further subterfuge was necessary. Mrs. Peters had not been smart enough to lie to me, instead tipping her hand immediately. She had the money, and she knew

that forty grand was not enough to entice
someone like me into letting her husband go,
so she was going to bring help with her when
she came. Here was the desperation. She was
going to do exactly what I had told her not to
do, and she was all but explaining to me that
this was so by admitting the truth when the lie
would have served her better.

That left Arthur Hands. I didn't know the
man, but I knew the kind. I'd seen it when I
was in the service. There were majors and
generals aplenty out there, all of whom thought
they knew the play, and every jack one of them
had a plan for how, with a crash and a bash and
a holler, we could penetrate enemy lines
straight to Berlin. And every one of them had a
man on their staff, a guy with small, black eyes,
whose sole use in this world was that he could
make hackneyed dreams come true. Those guys
had to go somewhere after the war, and they
returned to their old profession upon rotating
back to the free world. You saw them in the
employ of the rich and powerful, eyes as black
as ever, and hands all too willing to do the work
their masters' dare not.

Recall, then, that when Mort Peters' car
was fished from the bay that there had been a
body in it. A man like Peters would never sully
his hands in such a way. In fact, it took a
special kind of person, the black-eyed sort, who
could pull the trigger on such a thing. You had
to get very practical, far more even than that of

a widowed mother of three on Skid Row trying to make ends meet. You had to look past all the pleasant things about a person and find the ugliest. That meant you had to look for imperfections, the moles, the scars, the general stoop to the shoulders, all the things that we try to erase from our appearance, yet the very same things that give us our character.

Mort Peters was a vain man, as were most men in his position. He could never have found that man walking the streets, the one with a similar black mole on his jaw line, or the burn scar I had noticed on the hand that had taken my Zippo from me. A fellow like Arthur Hands could. He could find that person and track him for days, perhaps weeks, getting to know his every move, where he went with his best girl, the places he hung out with friends, what he liked for dinner, how much money he had in the bank, where he worked, whether he was Democrat or Republican, even how he shaved in the mornings. He could get to know such a fellow as intimately as a lover might, down to counting the hairs on the back of his head. He could come to see the man as something like a friend even, such was his knowledge of him, and in a different world, he would muse, the two might have been steadfast chums.

A guy like Arthur Hands could do all of that, and then, when the time came, he could put the snatch on the guy, haul him off to some place where single light bulbs dangled from long cords on the ceilings and swayed the light back and forth at the slightest disturbance. He could assure the guy that all would be well, and that soon he would be going home. He could share with him cigarettes, help him eat, clean him up, change his clothes, but then again, when the time came, he could also do other things. Like make a scar on his hand in case one hadn't been there in the first place, give it time to heal up and hair over, and then put the guy down for an eternal rest, all so his boss could pull the big con on his employers.

This was the kind of monster I was unleashing on Arlene and Muncey, not that they didn't deserve it.

I pretended to read the historical while I ate. This put further distance between me and Arlene, who I could feel was still watching me like a hawk. Even so, some sense of propriety kept her away from me, save to occasionally come by and fill my cup. The steady ebb and flow of customers did its part, too.

One of the guys at the counter left, but was quickly replaced by a salesman type in a checked suit and a ridiculous hat that looked like he was auditioning to be Red Skelton's stand-in. He brought his showcase in to try and work a few sales over a meal. Arlene let him know in no uncertain terms that soliciting in the diner was prohibited. The guy didn't lose his smile, but he desisted in selling toilet brushes. I took out a ballpoint pen from my pocket and began circling words in the historical.

A family of five came in, looking exhausted and harried. Their clothes had the look of having been slept in. They piled into the booth nearest the john and said nothing to each other. The man was ready to go ape. You could see it. There was such tension behind his eyes, you'd think he didn't have any organs left inside, just an endless amount of blood. If he hadn't struck his wife or one of the kids yet, he would, and soon. The wife's back was to me, but I could see by the slump of her shoulders she was trying to make herself as small as possible so maybe she escaped his attention. The children were just tired, and scared. They didn't understand why they were having to leave from wherever they came from and go wherever it was they were headed. They certainly didn't understand that it was their father's failure that was the cause, and so when he finally gave one of them the business, whether it be here or somewhere else, they wouldn't understand that, either. I felt a measure of sympathy.

Arlene brought them menus and said virtually nothing to them as she took their orders, only to ask the necessary questions.

I went to relieve myself, and when I came back two more men had come in to sit at the counter. One had struck up a conversation with the salesman about fiberglass bottom boats; the other sat reading the newspaper. As I returned to my seat, I heard the grumbling of a powerful engine pulling up. Outside, some young guy was hopping off a motorcycle. He was dressed in dark, denim jeans rolled up at the cuffs, sturdy boots, and a leather jacket. He had a leather bombardier's hat strapped to his head, but he immediately pulled this off to reveal a wild shock of hair that could have used a barber. He slapped a slouching cap over the top of it and swaggered inside, making a show of sidling over to a booth in such a way I was sure he must be a regular. Arlene gave no sign that she recognized him. Fresh kid, then. She'd love that.

When Arlene came to drop a menu he said, "Nah, don't bother with that, Mom. Gimme two eggs over easy, a pot of coffee, and some hashbrowns. I'm starved."

"You look it," Arlene snarled at him. He made a move like he was going to swat her rump as she walked past, but Arlene gave him a look that made him think otherwise.

He caught me staring and smiled. "She's just playing hard to get, huh?" he said, laughing. I smiled back at him. He looked maybe twenty, but the tattoo on his forearm when his sleeve rode up said otherwise. I'd seen a few during the war. He'd been in a carrier group, probably in the Pacific Theater. I put his age instead as a youthful thirty, maybe a few years younger.

He chewed a grubby nail and gave me a closer once-over. "Say, do I know you from somewhere?"

"I get that a lot. Where are you from?"

"Around. San Fran, mostly."

"Think billboards," I said.

His eyes lit up, and he snapped his fingers. "You're that guy! The detective!"

"Johnny Hardwood, of Hardwood, Smoller, and Tate."

"That is swell! You're a regular celebrity," he said.

"Now I don't get that a lot. You're all right, kid."

"Thanks. Hey, what're you doing this far upstate?"

I shrugged. "Just seeing what can be seen."

He winked at me. "Oh, I get it. Must be a big case."

"Getting bigger by the minute."

"Man, your kind of work must be exciting."

"Not really, no."

"Come on! On the level: it's bullets, broads, and bull malarkey, right?"

"Yeah, but there's little payout for that kind of thing. The real score is in working for big companies, and their kind of business isn't usually so glamorous. It's more sitting around in motel rooms, eating bad Chinese, and playing the waiting game."

He slid out of his booth and came to sit with me. I found this strangely similar to what I had experienced the day before with Mort Peters. He bummed my last cigarette off me, and I lit it with my Zippo. "You waiting on someone right now?" he asked me.

"Yes."

"Who?"

"Who else? A woman."

He winked at me again. Arlene brought him his food. She gave me a look. The guy started pouring ketchup over everything on his plate. I nodded at her that the kid was okay, and she took off back to the counter, where she went down the line, refilling coffee cups. I'd put the dime store novel in my coat pocket when I'd gone to the john, but I pulled it out now and set it down on the table.

"Am I interrupting your reading?" he asked.

"No, it's starting to chafe. Thought I'd set it down here."

"Any good?"

"It's not bad. I'm almost done with it, in fact. I'll let you have it when I'm done."

"Nah, that's all right. I'm not much of a reader."

"I wasn't, either, until I got drafted."

His eyebrows went up. "Where'd you serve?"

"I Company, 354th Infantry. I was in a mortar squad."

He nodded but said nothing. A semi pulling a load of logs headed south parked across the way, and a grizzly bear of a man stomped up. Arlene looked happy to see him, and he made a loud production of entering and giving her a hug. He grabbed a booth, and Arlene followed him over with a menu. They spent more time jawing than him ordering, so I imagined he was one of those kinds who was a regular in every place he stopped.

I took that opportunity to knock my coffee cup onto the floor. It hit and shattered louder than anyone could have imagined, myself included, and everyone in the room jumped. Faces turned to me, and I smiled and held up my hands to say sorry. Arlene made to come and see, but I waved her off.

"My mistake. I'll clean it up."

Arlene looked like she didn't want me anywhere near the counter, but before she could say anything the truck driver started in again, saying a few uncharitable things about his employer, and the likelihood of whether he was going to even bother making this particular run on-schedule or not. With her back turned, I slipped behind the counter.

"Hey, while you're back there, how's about a refill?" the salesman asked, grinning.

"Sorry, buddy, I'm off the clock."

I knelt and found a neatly stacked pile of rags beneath the countertop that Arlene no doubt used to wipe everything down. I grabbed one and gave it all a once-over. A baseball bat was on the bottom shelf. This looked like a Muncey-style peacekeeper to me, something used only if a guy got out of line. Next to it was a Swiss Army knife and a carton of Lucky

Strikes. I copped a pack of those and was about to go back to the table when something else caught my eye. I peered in, realizing that I was now taking too long and would soon start to arouse suspicion.

Back behind the pile of rags was a familiar sight. The shoulder holster with my service .45 had been tucked behind. Being to the side of the pile I could now see it. I wanted to check on Arlene's progress, but I couldn't chance it. Even if she didn't notice me, if I went poking my head up to look around, someone at the counter would see me acting suspiciously and might tell her. After all, they didn't know me from Adam. I could be some schmuck trying to rip off an honest, hard-working gal like Arlene, and they'd never be the wiser. I left the .45 but nicked the knife and got back to my booth as quickly as possible, grabbing a broom and dustpan as I went. I swept up the remains of the cup and wiped the floor down with the clean rag. Arlene came by, glaring at me as she went.

"I suppose you'll want a new cup o' Joe, huh?"

"Thought I might drink some floor polish instead," I said. "It would probably taste better."

The salesman and the gentleman talking to him overheard us and chuckled.

"I can arrange that," Arlene said, and snatched the broom and dustpan out of my hands.

I sat down again. My new friend had already inhaled his breakfast. The remains of it were pushed to the side. The paperback was gone. He was drinking his coffee and smiling.

"That gal is a class act," he said.

"Of that, I'm sure," I replied. "You must be hungry."

His eyes never left mine. "Yeah. Famished."

"Watch out for the cook. He's a big guy, strong as a bull and mean as a snake. And he likes to overseason his chicken. There's no talking to him about it."

"Good to know. If that's the case, maybe I'll mosey on down the trail some. Sacramento's not far away, right?"

"You'll get there before lunch."

"Good to know. Hey, Mister Hardwood, thanks. It's been swell."

"Good to meet you, kid," I said. I stuck out a hand, and he shook it.

"Think I'll hit the trail soon as well. I'll wait for this coffee to run through me and visit the john before going. Half an hour, I should be back on the road."

"Where you headed?"

"Same place you are, as soon as I'm done here."

The smile got bigger. "That's just fine. Maybe I'll see you around."

"Anything's possible."

The kid left. He hopped on his chopper and

started it up with a considerable sound and fury. The windows rattled, and soon he was speeding off into the distance. Arlene brought me a new cup of coffee, and I drank it. I smoked one more cigarette for good measure and considered what I had to do next. It was just past noon by then. No one was expecting anything until the afternoon. Mrs. Peters wasn't supposed to arrive until then. I could see by Arlene's manner she was tense. By the way she'd handled Mort and me the day before, it was clear she was no apprentice in the art of shanghaiing travelers. Only, there had never been a payoff like this before. Try as she might to keep her pragmatic head about her, bags of loot were starting to trickle into her peripheral vision. Pretty soon her hands would start to shake. By dinner rush she would screw up an order or two, this from a woman who probably did this job in her sleep.

Muncey I wasn't so sure about. A different set of things got his kettle whistling. By the way he'd jumped the gun with Mort, he apparently had a short fuse, though the guy I'd seen thus far was pretty level-headed. What I knew about real psychopaths was that they were nice guys until they weren't. That sounded about right. Anybody loved money, but I think for Muncey it was the infliction of pain. Maybe he was starting to get antsy, too, thinking about lying in wait for Arthur Hands to show his cards. I couldn't say what went on in a mind like that, if he anticipated the kill or not, or if he just did it. Any way you sliced it, I had them out of their normal routine. I also had them where I wanted them, at least for the time being. Now I had to make things worse for them, really throw a monkey wrench into their plans.

I waited a while and then went back to the john. I'd made sure to make frequent trips throughout the morning, so that if I went more than once in an hour Arlene would not suspect it. I was banking on her putting together my intestinal discomfort from yesterday and my trips today as part of the same problem, and that was Muncey's cooking. Let her think I couldn't handle it. Arrogance can mimic feelings of trust if you think someone is weak or too afraid to cross you.

I took care of business and slipped the Swiss Army knife from my pocket. There was a machine bolted to the wall near the sink with a roll of linen cloth hanging from it that could rotate occasionally so a guy could dry his hands. I slit the cloth and pulled it free and tossed it and all the spare toilet paper I could find into a pile by the door. After making certain I'd left nothing in any of the pockets I took off my suit coat and tossed it into the pile for good measure. I pulled my Zippo, flicked it twice, lit the pile in several places to get it going, and I ducked out.

Arlene was so busy then that she apparently failed to notice I was now in shirtsleeves. I sat down at my table, but this time I didn't sip my coffee or light another cigarette. I tried not to think about what was coming next, or if I was walking out of this joint on my own power or being dragged out by the coroner. I'd had enough of that kind of thinking already.

A dish fell and broke in the kitchen. Arlene's head snapped up. Mine did the same. She looked at me then, and I stared back. We were both thinking the same thing. She put down her dish rag and started toward the kitchen when the truck driver friend of Arlene's yelled over the crowd:

"Hey, Arlene, you got smoke coming from underneath this door!"

All heads turned to look. Arlene stopped in her tracks to crane her head above the boys at the counter.

"What?" she asked.

"Smoke. Something's wrong in your restroom."

"Well, I don't—"

She never finished the sentence. What sounded like a whole rack of dishes crashed in the kitchen, but then the mother of the destitute family shrieked "Fire!" and that started an exodus into the parking lot. Arlene and I exchanged glances, and she started toward the swinging door at the back of the building. I could see gray smoke starting to peek from beneath the doorjamb.

"Muncey, come running!" she howled and plunged through the bathroom door. A second later she stuck her head back out again, let loose a cough, and said to me, "Hardwood, you stay out here and keep your eyes peeled. You hear?"

I climbed to my feet. "Will do, Arlene."

She disappeared. I looked toward the kitchen, but there was no sign of Muncey anywhere. I had an idea of what was transpiring, but I couldn't worry about that just then. The others had run to the side of the building near the john to get a glimpse of the small window in the restroom that was no doubt now pouring smoke. Everyone loves a fire, after all. I used that as a cover to get behind the counter and grab the baseball bat and .45. Arlene was a fool not to take something with her. My intention was to make her pay for that oversight.

Chapter Six

When I found her in the john, she was spewing a string of obscenities I would have thought only a sailor could manage, and the pipes groaned as she had the tap wide open to throw water on the flames. I eased inside and let the door fall closed behind me. She didn't hear me coming, but she nevertheless happened to turn at the moment I made my entrance. Her face was streaked with tears from the smoke, and there were black runners of mascara coursing down her cheeks.

She showed me a mouth full of teeth. "What's the big idea, Hardwood?" she asked.

I showed her the bat as a reply.

The time for talk was over. I let her have it upside the head. Her jaw raced ahead of the rest of her face as it snapped to the side. She fell backward onto the smoking remains of the fire I'd set, and a handful of teeth skittered across the floor toward the toilet, leaving bloody, little trails behind them. I felt bad about that. The rational part of me knew I could have taken her without violence. By then even a hard case like Arlene had to know the play was in motion, and she'd been caught unawares. But instead I gave her another one across the back of the head when she tried to rise up off the floor. The savage somewhere inside me said she had it coming for making me afraid for my life.

I exited the john and made for the kitchen. The sounds of things breaking, punctuated by the occasional grunt and curse, were still evident. I was about to push my way in and pay the same respects to Muncey that I had with Arlene when I got another idea. I went out the front and ducked around the opposite side of the building from where everyone had gathered to watch the fire. Somebody was pulling away just as I was coming out. I could only presume they were going to rouse whatever passed for a fire department this far out in the sticks.

I found them squaring off with one another. Muncey was breathing hard, his big, bald head bathed in sweat. His left bicep was bleeding from a stab wound that had gone clean through the muscle. He held a meat cleaver in one hand, and a switch knife in the other. It didn't look like mine, which meant he'd taken it in the struggle. The kid looked a lot worse for wear. One eye was closing up on him, and he had blood trickling out of his mouth. He, too, looked like he'd just run a marathon. Muncey turned an eye on me and grinned.

"You showed up just in time to see me filet this greasy, little shrimp," he said. His smile was missing a tooth. "Came for us just like you said, Hardwood. I gotta hand it to you. Just wish you'd been right about the hour, is all."

"He's maybe a little too ambitious," I replied. "I hope you don't mind, but I helped myself to the bat when I heard the stuff breaking."

"We got the girl?"

"Yeah, Arlene's on her."

"What's she like?"

"How do you think? She's hysterical. Thinks we're going to ice her, too."

"Maybe we will."

The kid threw a punch so fast it looked like

it had wings on it. He dotted Muncey in his left eye, and he followed it up with two jabs to the solar plexus. A guy like Muncey, though, it was like punching a mountain. The eye watered up on him, sure, but the subsequent blows did nothing but make him angrier. He slashed with the meat cleaver, but the kid ducked under it, which made the switch knife useless as well. Muncey tried to bum rush him, then, but the kid was too quick and kept pace with him. Muncey didn't push him all the way across the room and against the sink where he couldn't backpedal anymore, and that was a mistake. The kid was going to duck under the next attack, and then Muncey's back would be to me. I decided to move before I lost my position.

I came up behind Muncey and drove the bat into his kidney. He bellowed like I'd tricked him into a slaughterhouse. The kid caught him with a couple of good shots to the face. Muncey threw an elbow back at me, but I'd danced out as soon as I'd connected with the first shot. Once the arm dropped I was back in again, and this time I caught him with a blow to the ribs. My footing was bad, though, and I slipped on the broken dishes. His wind left him a little, but he recovered enough to spin around and nearly cut me in two with the meat cleaver. Luckily, I was falling out of the way when he did it and only got a scratch on the side. The kid jumped on Muncey's back and tried to wrestle the switch knife out of his hand. That gave me the time I needed to find my footing and move back to attack. Muncey's eyes were wild now. He knew the game was up, but he wasn't going to be beaten so easily as Arlene. He slashed twice at me with the cleaver, growled when the kid bit him on the forearm, and told me in no uncertain terms what he was going to do to me when he got me.

That's when he got smart. He dropped the switch knife, and the kid, focused more on that than his own safety, went for it. When he did Muncey snatched him up like a sack of potatoes and tossed him across the room. The kid crashed into the trash can, and garbage went everywhere.

"Just you and me now," Muncey said to me.

"Were you ever going to let me go?" I asked him.

Muncey said nothing. Instead, he gave me a gap-toothed smile and showed me the cleaver. I supposed that was my answer.

It was his game, then. I waited for him to attack, and he didn't waste much time in doing so. He came at me fast, faster than you'd think a guy that big could move. I could tell he was confident of his chances of getting me in the bum rush. I was nearly in a corner, but I still had the bat, too. I waited for the attack, and rather than counterattack I swung the bat at the meat cleaver, not trying to block the weapon, but to strike the hand that was holding it. It was a risky move, but it paid off. The inside swing wasn't my hardest, but Muncey's attack was clumsy, probably from his punctured bicep. The bat cracked his fingers, and he yelled, dropped the cleaver, and went wholeheartedly in rushing me.

I got a whiff of bad cologne as he put a shoulder into my gut and drove me back against the wall. A crock of flour fell off a shelf overhead and covered us. I got in two decent shots, but Muncey had me. He lifted me by my neck. At first he didn't squeeze. He seemed to like the idea of having me at his mercy, squirming, trying to break free, but knowing I couldn't get out of that iron death trap he called a hand.

"I'm gonna rip you open and read my future," Muncey said. "You understand me, Hardwood? They're never gonna find you because there won't be anything left to find."

"They'll find what's left of Arlene, sure enough."

I don't know why I had that moment of bravado. The words just seemed to slip out before my mouth could police them. If Muncey had me, I wanted him to know that I'd been the one to ship his girlfriend. It certainly had an effect. Muncey's eyes reduced to slits on his face. A vein stood out on his forehead, and that's about the last I remembered for a little while, as he clamped down on my throat and began crushing the life out of me.

A death struggle is a curious thing. For the

two locked in it, the time stretches out towards infinity. I'd heard stories of a guy bleeding out from a sliced artery in his leg still having the time and wherewithal to kill three guys before he dropped. Three people in thirty seconds. They never feel like seconds. Muncey had me in a grip, and it was taking forever to kill me, or so it seemed to me. I couldn't draw breath, and my body, free of rational control, was flailing about in an effort to get free. If I'd had control of myself a well-placed kick might have done the trick, but a lack of oxygen had put me in a different place mentally. Black spots were creeping into my vision. Soon I would black out, and I imagined then what it would be like to never wake up again. Such speculation isn't good for a guy like me, but I supposed I wasn't like many other guys in my profession. That was why I had gotten locked into a death struggle in the first place, and it was why I was going to die in the middle of nowhere with very little to show for it. Other guys in my place, they would have played it a lot smarter, but then again, was I really a detective, or just playing one until another gig came along?

Muncey grunted suddenly, and his grip on me loosened. I dropped to the floor in time to see the kid behind him, switch knife in his hand, and he was stabbing Muncey in the kidney over and over, as fast as he could. The fist holding the knife was bloody. Muncey turned on him and caught him with two good shots to the face, but you could tell the lacerated kidney was already starting to affect him. He drove the kid back against the wall and worked his ribs over, but the punches were getting sluggish and weaker. The kid didn't have much left, either. He was beaten and bruised, and I could see a red stain spreading across his shirt and down the side of his denims that I hadn't noticed before. I lay there and waited to catch my breath while the two of them hashed it out.

Muncey finally got smart and got the kid around the throat. The kid's eyes went wide immediately, and it was clear Muncey had enough gas left in the tank to finish the job. I picked myself up and grabbed the bat off the ground. The meat cleaver lay nearby, but I preferred the bat. I walked up behind Muncey, not caring if he heard me coming or not. He was dying; he knew it. There wasn't going to be any getting out of this. He just wanted to finish one of us before his time came. I wasn't going to let that happen. I hit him across the back of the head, and he snapped forward. He released the kid, who dropped to the ground much as I had a few moments before. I stood over Muncey and watched him breathe.

"Finish it," the kid said through a series of gasps.

I did what I was told. I hit Muncey four more times across the head until I was sure he would never get up again.

The kid struggled to his feet. He nodded his
thanks at me.

"Arthur Hands, I presume?" I asked.

"Yeah."

"Johnny Hardwood."

"So you said."

"Your employer is dead."

"Yeah. I figured as much."

"I thought I told you to wait."

He grinned at me. "Maybe I didn't read
that part of your book."

"Maybe you should've. We could have
taken Muncey at the same time."

Arthur Hands shook his head. "It's like you
said: Mr. Peters is dead. This guy had it coming
to him. Coming from me."

I gestured to the wound at his side. "How's
that?"

He was woozy as he said, "I, uh, I need to
get somewhere."

I helped him stay on his feet. We left by the
back door. The crowd was still around the front,
so no one saw us take the path from the diner
to the small trailer in the woods behind it. I got
the door open and Hands inside, where I laid
him on Muncey and Arlene's bed. I found a
clean towel in the bathroom and used it to put
pressure on the wound, hoping to stop the
bleeding before he got too far gone.
Sacramento was too far away, and anyway I
had no idea where my keys or Mort's might be.
Hands probably wouldn't survive the search, so

I had to make sure he was stabilized before I could proceed.

The irony of that moment was not lost on me. Here was a guy who was no doubt coming to kill me, as well as Arlene and Muncey, who I had made before he could start any trouble. I knew he'd be coming first, and so I'd circled words in the dimestore novel explaining my plan. Where I had no words for things like "Mort" I'd circled individual letters in words to spell it out. I'd also explained what I planned to do, which was create a diversion so we could get out of there, call the cops before either Muncey or Arlene knew what was going on, and have them arrested for extortion and murder. The extortion charge wouldn't stick because it had been my plan, but it sounded so good on paper I was sure Hands would fall for it.

But did I think for a moment it was going down like that? No. Never. Hands was never letting me get away. I knew too much about the scam he and the Peters were playing with All-American's money. The switch knife he'd used on Muncey had probably had my name on it first. I knew also that if he lived, Hands was going to find a way to get even with me, eventually. Guys like him didn't like loose ends, and they didn't like getting beaten, either. But I couldn't just sit by and let him buy it, not if I could make a difference.

He was still conscious, at least for the time

being, so I decided to find out what I could while I still had him lucid.

"So where's Mrs. Peters?"

He smiled. "Which one?"

"The one you don't want the cops to know about."

"Somewhere no one can get her."

Good. That meant she wasn't here, with him. That told me exactly what I needed to know. There was never going to be an exchange. They were going for the home run, getting Mort back, and keeping the loot. That had probably been Hands' idea, unless I had completely misread Mrs. Peters.

"How did Mort go?" he asked me.

"The big guy. Muncey. I imagine he was beaten to death. I never saw it. They had me trussed up elsewhere."

"Terrible way to go."

"You don't sound too broke up over it."

Hands said nothing. I'd put two and two together by then, anyway, at least where his loyalty lay. If so, I'd misread him as well.

"So who was the guy in Mort's car, the one the cops fished out of the lake?"

"Why do you want to know?"

"So I can send his family an anonymous letter. Let them know not to expect him home anytime soon."

Hands nodded. "I thought about doing that."

"Why? That would blow your boss' cover

and put you in line for a murder charge if you were found out."

Hands said nothing, just stared at me from his good eye. Now I did have the whole picture.

"Does she know anything about your big plan?"

"No. And please don't tell her, neither."

"It's not my story to tell. If she wants to pay my salary, I'll give it to her, all wrapped up in a bow, but I doubt I'm ever going to see the faux Mrs. Peters in the flesh."

"Nah. She's a pretty smart girl, Hardwood. You wouldn't know it to talk to her, but she's got smarts, that kid."

"I'm sure she does," I said, but Hands had already lost consciousness.

Chapter Seven

The bleeding eventually stopped, and I cleaned up in the kitchen sink. I was in rough shape, but I'd live. It took twenty minutes of primping like some schoolgirl ballerina before I looked human enough to go see what was happening at the diner. By then the uproar was in full swing. Somewhere along the way someone had discovered Arlene, for the children of the indigent family were in tears when I arrived, and their mother, also weeping, was consoling them. The men were standing around, looking hostile, as men often do to appear useful. The truck driver, upon seeing me in my ragged state, pointed a finger at me.

"There he is!" The hostile eyes turned in my direction.

"What do you know about all this? You were the last one out of there."

This was the salesman. All of a sudden he'd turned from clown to inquisitor.

"Yeah, I know a thing or two about it," I replied.

He didn't seem too happy with me. "You got some big idea about smashing women?"

I'd found my ID in the trailer, along with my car keys, and I pulled the wallet out to show them. "Have the police been called?" I asked.

"Yeah, they're on their way," the truck driver said. "You got some explaining to do when they get here."

"And I will," I said. "What I won't do is answer to you. You're all witnesses. No one leaves until they get here."

"I got to be in Salem by tonight," he said.

"That's between you and the cops," I replied. "But unless you want trouble the next time you're through, I'd suggest you play ball."

No one was happy with me, but I didn't care. I went and leaned against my Chevy to smoke a cigarette and wait for the cops. The truck driver glared at me through the window until he realized he wasn't going to get a rise out of me. A couple of patrol units pulled into the diner parking lot a few minutes later. A meat wagon came soon after.

I was soon introduced to Officer Kerns, who was not happy with me, either. You could tell he had taken respite a time or two at Herbie's Diner, as he was disinclined to believe me about Arlene or Muncey's guilt. I gave him a full rundown of the past two days: shadowing Mort Peters, the abduction, the plan to lure my suspects into the plot and play them off Arlene and Muncey, the case for All-American, and the subsequent fights. I held nothing back, regardless of how it might make me look.

I didn't want anyone to get an idea I was holding something back, not when it had been me who had proposed the extortion plot to begin with. I think what saved me there was that I had never intended for the plot to go through, and there was no way they could prove otherwise.

Kerns wasn't impressed and was obviously going to try and pin the whole thing on me if he could. He especially didn't like what I had done in convincing my captors not to kill me. I'd put other people in danger, he said, and that was irresponsible, reckless, but what he was really telling me was that he was sore at me for living when I should have let his buddies field-dress me in some hidden grove. The two poor, innocent folk I had endangered were involved in embezzlement, money laundering, insurance fraud, tax evasion, and murder, but I had the handlebar mustache and black cloak.

His associate, a fat Pole named Gorka, was a little more sympathetic. He made a few phone calls from the diner and established my bona fides with Detective O'Quinn, an officer in L.A. who had worked with me a time or two. Kerns grimaced at this and demanded evidence. I showed them to the beat-up blue Ford registered under the last name Carter. They popped the trunk and found the remains of Mort Peters, now in a progressive state of decay from being locked in a trunk in the middle of a California summer. Kerns called this circumstantial, and by now was sizing me up for a double, maybe triple, homicide. I mentioned Arlene's connection with the theatre scene. Gorka went to check on that, too, and came back with more good news. Roderick "Muncey" Carter was currently wanted for questioning in two unsolved homicides in Los Angeles. Senior detective in charge of the case: Detective Allan O'Quinn. My luck couldn't have been any better than if I had written it myself. That was a nice change after the time I'd had.

Kerns couldn't hold me, not even for questioning since I had come clean about my involvement. He did threaten to start proceedings to have my license revoked in California, but I wasn't worried. If it came to pass, it came to pass. There was nothing I could do about it. Gorka offered his hand to shake.

He considered what I'd done to be gutsy, and I'd nabbed a whole slew of bad guys in the process.

"They should do a movie about you, kid," he said to me.

The irony of that wasn't lost on me.

Muncey was dead when the boys in white found him. He'd bled out from multiple lacerations to his kidney. The subsequent autopsy would reveal bleeding into his brain as well, which would also have caused him to expire, probably before help could arrive. Arlene was alive, with five missing teeth, a broken jaw, and a massive concussion. They rushed her to Sacramento, and Kerns followed them, leaving Gorka to clean up.

I showed Gorka to the trailer behind the diner, but there was no sign of Hands, just blood stains on the mattress and a roll of used duct tape covered in red fingerprints. There was a blood trail that went off into the woods. Gorka promised they would get dogs on the trail before long, but I had a pretty good idea they wouldn't find any sign of him.

That made things difficult for me. My face was all over. The rent on the billboard was paid through the middle of next year, courtesy of the smash-and-grab crew from which it had originated. What was free publicity for me was also an invitation for Hands to try and punch my ticket at his leisure, assuming he lived. I resolved to consider my options on that once

I'd wrapped up this case. I certainly couldn't spend the next two to five years looking over my shoulder all the time, and guys like Hands, as I've said, are patient. He may not have shown it where Muncey was concerned, but that was because a woman was involved. Women were always good for taking a man out of character.

By sundown the police no longer had any use for me. Gorka had questioned all the witnesses, one by one, and let them go. Apart from the truck driver making half-attempts at a claim that Arlene had begged him to save her from me, there were no real surprises. Gorka pressed the guy on the matter, and he backed down quickly enough.

All the long drive back to Los Angeles I thought about how I planned to find the studio's money. There was still that to consider. Forty grand of it at least was out of my reach, short of calling in a solid from a swami with a yin for telelocating blondes with eiderdown for brains. The rest may or may not have been invested in any number of films, from one to a hundred. Following that paper trail, assuming there was one, could take months or days, depending on how sly the cover-up. Then there would be the matter of litigating the return of the money, which could take forever. My part in it was about to end, whether I found it or not, so I wasn't all that concerned, but like anyone, I liked a nice, tight ending to a story. It's just that, in this business, it rarely works out that way.

Back in the city I found a phone directory and looked up Malibu-69755. The address listed it off Paseo Canyon Drive. Being tired and beat up didn't matter to me. I stopped at a place on a cross-street just off Rodeo, an all-night diner of all places, and got a cup of coffee to keep me awake. Afterward I made the rest of the journey.

The home was modest given the obvious tastes of its owners. I found a key under the doormat and let myself inside. The interior had a nice but sparse décor, a lot of whites and creams except the bathroom, which was a jarring scarlet. It was neat but lived-in, and very quiet. I didn't expect to find anyone home and was not surprised to find only a few lady's garments left hanging askew in the master bedroom's closet. The remains of dinner were lying unwashed in the kitchen sink. That told me the faux Mrs. Peters had probably left just after my phone call. Wherever she was now, I hoped she was enjoying her money.

Off a hallway that ran the length of the place, I found a small office with a masculine décor. Here no doubt was Peters' sanctum on what I could only assume were his rare visits home. There was a heavy oak desk standing by the window with its chair knocked over. Beneath the desk I found a floor safe that had been left open. Whatever had once been inside was now gone. I rifled through the drawers and found nothing, no notes, stationery, or anything that might tell me where Peters had put his money. A small metal filing cabinet yielded nothing as well. They'd even been so careful as to clean out the wastebasket before fleeing.

Having nowhere better to look I tried the backyard. I found nothing but an old garage that was filled with junk I imagined belonged to whoever had owned the place before the Peters. I just couldn't see Mort Peters in a dirty, dusty place like that, dressed in a cardigan and smoking a pipe as he scraped rust off his tools with a wire brush. Maybe I'd had him wrong, too. I'd certainly misread Hands' motivations, and apparently the guile of Mrs. Peters as well. It would not have surprised me at all to find there were pieces of Mort Peters that didn't fit my preconceived notions, either.

I left the garage feeling more than a bit crestfallen for having come up empty-handed. I decided maybe I would go home, grab a few hours' sleep, and then come back later, when I caught sight of a couple of trashcans overstuffed with trash near the back door. Having nothing better to do, I grabbed a couple of the bags off the top and took them inside, where I upended them on the kitchen floor for a better look. If I'd been looking for keepsakes and memories, I would have hit the jackpot, as I found photos of the Peters, ornate picture frames, a baseball signed by someone with an illegible autograph, and a framed high school diploma of Deborah McGonickle, dated five years ago. I checked the photos and found a beautiful blonde girl who fit the age.

"So, Mrs. Peters, we meet at last," I said. I decided to keep one photo and the diploma. If All-American wanted to track her down, they could use this. If they offered me the job, I would even take it, but as far as I was concerned, that was outside the current scope of my investigations.

Four bags upended yielded next to nothing but a pile of filthy trash on the kitchen floor. I had one left and was tempted to leave it, but for the sake of thoroughness I pulled it from the can and tossed it on the floor. It was heavier and its contents more solid. I opened this one and removed a box. It was the correct size for a standard eight-and-a- half-by-eleven letter page. The box was blue and black with stately gold letters that read BurnsFolio in swirling calligraphy. The box yielded stationery for a company called Abramowitz & Englehart. It was good, heavy stock, official-looking and professional. Beneath the masthead was an address in tiny, cerulean blue script that listed offices in Hollywood. If the address actually existed, I would eat my hat. I took one of the pieces of stationery, folded it in eighths, and stuck it in my pants pocket, next to the .45, which I'd never gotten around to firing, even when my life had been in danger. Some days, I didn't feel like I was very good at my job and would one day wind up on a slab somewhere, dead from a very stupid wound to a part of my anatomy that would only get me laughed at by the coroner.

I drove home and got five hours of sleep before dragging myself to a telephone to call my contact at All-American, a gee named Levine. His secretary told me he was out, and I left a message. My call was returned within five minutes.

"Hardwood." Levine had a nervous, schmoozy voice. I pictured a guy who bathed in Brylcreem, and I probably wasn't far off the mark. "What have you got for me?"

I told him about Peters and the setup. He never made a squeak about any of it, good or bad. For a guy like Levine, Peters was always a dead or alive scenario, and he didn't care how the guy came home, just as long as he came home. The money was what he cared about. He asked about it as soon as he could manage a respectable murmur of empathy for the deceased.

"I can't be for sure on this," I said, "but your people can check up on it easily enough. I found reams of stationery in Peters' home office for a dummy firm called Abramowitz & Engelhart. Check your records first, but if it doesn't pan out, put the word out with the other studios to check their ledgers. His accomplice, a girl named Deborah McGonickle, told me Peters had invested the stolen money in one or several films hoping for a bigger windfall. The idea then was that they would take the money and disappear."

Levine let fly with a stream of obscenities peppered with Yiddish curses. I'd been floored by Peters' brass, myself, so I could sympathize.

"Do you have any idea how hard it's going to be to back the money out of a project, especially if it's in bed with one of our competitors?" Levine asked me.

"I would imagine that was his plan. It was a victory for him if he could pull it off, and he could make a nightmare for you if he got caught. Either way, I feel like he had the whole thing sewed up pretty tight."

"You sound like you liked the guy."

"Impressed is more like it. By the way, when you find the money you're going to want to earmark a portion of it and cut a cashier's check made out to Deborah Peters. You'll call me when that happens."

"Who's she?"

"Peters' real wife. She's in a bad way, financially, and his life insurance policy is tied up with your money. She could really use a payday to get her on her feet again. I'd like to see to that personally."

"I'll see that it's done."

"Good."

"And I guess we should start talking about your paycheck as well."

"Nothing to talk about," I replied. "The amount we agreed on stands. I want nothing more and expect you to honor your end of the deal, regardless of how this turns out. You'll get a bill from me by the end of the week along with a copy of my expense report."

"That's fine. Listen, I want you to know we appreciate what you've done for us, Hardwood. No one's going to forget it, either. In fact, if you were to send us a head shot we could see about getting you signed on to a contract. How does that sound?"

"I'll think about it."

Levine chuckled an oily chuckle. "So much for not wanting more, hey?"

"You're right," I said. "Keep the contract."

"What?" That was not the reaction Levine had expected. "You can't be serious."

"Completely. If I came in, I'd want to pick my project, and I know that's not going to happen. Besides, I'm getting past my prime, and anyway, it could be I'm only good to play private eyes and heavies anymore. I'm not sure I want to go back to that."

We talked it over a while longer, mostly because Levine couldn't give it up, me turning down the offer to come and work for one of the biggest studios in town. I did want it, but like a film from a while back said, I wanted it on my terms. I didn't want favors, and I didn't want to bump some kid who might be better suited to a role just because I suddenly had an in. That had happened to me, and I didn't want that kind of misery visited upon anyone else, just for my benefit.

After I hung up with Levine I slept three more hours. I woke groggy and with a headache. I took a powder for my head and made a pot of coffee to wash it down. A curious thought struck me as I finished my third cup. I went to the hall closet by the front door and dug through the junk inside until I found the dusty Clark Nova typewriter I'd bought for seventy-five cents at a resale shop in San Diego. I took it into my living room and set the machine heavily upon the coffee table in front of me, blew the dust off it, and made sure it was in proper working order. The P key stuck and had to be manually released when struck, but other than that, it was in fair shape. The ribbon was still fresh. I grabbed a piece of paper and ran it through the feed. I typed a cover page with my real name on it and gave it a title: MURDER BY THE ROADSIDE.

I pulled the page and fed a fresh sheet in. In the war I'd spent some time at regimental HQ as assistant quartermaster, not in a mortar squad as I'd told Hands. There, I'd learned to type pretty well, writing reports. When I'd rotated home, and the acting jobs had started to dry up, I'd bought the typewriter with the idea of becoming a screenwriter instead, just to stay in the business and maybe make a few bucks turning out melodramas.

90

Nothing had ever come of it, and when the Hardwood, Smoller, and Tate job came along, I put the typewriter in storage, making my literary ambitions a distant memory. But talking with Levine had me thinking of giving it another try. This could be my way of making it, I thought, of making it on my own terms. Detective films were big news, had been for some time. That well wasn't likely to dry up anytime soon, and I had a wealth of knowledge I could draw on. I'd start with my most recent job and the incident at Herbie's Diner. Get it all together while the impressions were still fresh, and I wouldn't have to fabricate ideas later that might sound false to the ear. The past two days had certainly been outlandish enough without requiring the audience to suspend too much of their disbelief. Tough-as-nails waitresses, giant short-order cooks, and boyish psychopaths dressed as biker hoodlums were already pushing things quite a bit.

I typed "FADE IN" and stared at the page until my vision got blurry. Where to begin?— that was the question. Did I start it with my initial phone call with Levine, only leave out the weeks of legwork that had gone into my finally locating Peters, or did I jump straight to the diner itself? In media res, it was called. I had a book on writing around somewhere, written by some gee who'd been in the pulps for years and wanted to go legitimate with a how-to-do-it guide. I'd found the term there. It

meant "in the middle of the action." That's
where you were supposed to start your work, if
possible. That made sense. Don't give the
audience any time to calm down, just start
hitting them with scene upon scene as fast as I
could manage it, make the dialogue snappy,
and give it a good bare knuckle brawl at the end.
No knives or the like. That was too messy. And
there had to be a girl in it, a love interest.
Maybe my character could get the girl, the faux
Mrs. Peters, Deborah McGonickle. That didn't
seem like such a long shot, not in the movies.

I sat there for an hour, just like that. My
hands never touched the keys, just sat folded in
my lap, with me perched on the edge of the
couch, like I was ready for action the moment
the muse struck me full in the face with
inspiration. It should be easy, I said, more to
comfort myself than anything. It'd just
happened to you. Just write what happened,
and it's practically a blank check from a studio
to run with it. Come on, Hardwood. It's never
going to get any easier than this.

My hands still didn't move. I stared at
them, and suddenly, up from my chest came a
chuckle. The chuckle became a guffaw, the
guffaw became a barking laugh, and the bark
became waves of hysterical laughter. Tears
rolled down my cheeks, and I held my sides as
they began to ache. I lay down and continued
to yuk it up, not knowing where it came from or
how I could stop it.

I rolled over onto my back and managed to catch my breath between bouts of breaking down again. Finally, with my eyes watery and my vision blurred I stared up at my ceiling. The laughter died away, replaced by a simple smile, the first real one I'd had in a long, long time.

"Who'm I kidding?" I whispered, then went out for a pack of cigarettes.

Bonus Story –
Hearts Full of Midnight

Chapter One

There's a quality to the night the eye can't escape. No matter how dark it seems, there's always light. Maybe just a little, but it's there. Even when the Moon is playing hide-and-seek, and an overcast sky has hidden the stars, there's still light somewhere in the universe where you can find your way.

It's man who robs the world of light. For millennia we've built, and lived in, boxes that trap the dark so neatly and so perfectly. It stands to reason that we'd eventually construct a thing that, when it goes off, it's brighter than the Sun. It feeds our need for opposition, for balance. Heat where it's cold, cold where it's hot. Breeze when it's stuffy; calm for all the noise living creates. Consider then that a home can be black as pitch when there's no love in it. Same with a marriage. Ideas as wholesome and warm as a home or wedded bliss turn out to be the best boxes of all, able to trap the absence of light and hold it prisoner. A perfect dark.

I'd like to say I considered all this in that

moment there in the living room, but it didn't come to me until sometime later. I never get deep or philosophical without a bottle of bourbon to drive me to the shindig, and I never stay long at the party, even when I go.

Instead, I watched Sally Burgess from across the tiny living room of that shoebox apartment, her standing between me and the window facing the empty alleyway, and I marveled at how she could cast a silhouette onto something as black as night.

Or how the nighttime could still glint off the nickel-plated .38 she was turning over in her hands, like she was trying to figure out which was the business end and who she wanted in front of it when the gun went off. I imagine it was the same way for our boys when they were building the other thing, the one whose light dwarfs suns. Who gets it, so the world can know it exists?

"Sally?" My throat hurt when I spoke, a delayed effect of having a giant maniac wrap his mitts around you and squeeze. Hard to believe, it'd only been a few days since I'd been fighting for my life, and now this. The distance between the two felt like years.

"Mrs. Burgess? You should be careful with that. I can hear the bullets clicking in the cylinders when you move it. It's loaded."

"Of course, it is," she replied. She hadn't been nearly choked to death, but the words weren't coming out of her throat any easier than they did mine, just for different reasons. Her back was to me, turned just enough to her left that I could catch a glimpse of what she held but still obscuring her face from me.

"Denton keeps it like that for protection," I continued. "Sure, he would. A piece doesn't have much use if someone breaks in, and you have to load it before you start shooting."

She said nothing. Her eyes were lost in the .38 and what it meant.

"But that doesn't mean it has to be used," I went on. I inched a step or two in her direction. Not too much; I couldn't be sure that she wouldn't turn the gun onto me if it came to it. That was enough to keep me hesitant. "There's plenty of firearms out there that have never been fired, you know. It's one of the few tools in the world that works better if it's never used."

I kept up this way, and the tone of my voice lulled her. She let me get close, approach her the way a husband might approach his wife, to wrap his arms around her waist when she's busy with the dishes or dinner. Instead of stealing kisses, I reached out with my good arm and took the gun from her hands. Slowly, real easy-like. I brushed her shoulder, and my forearm felt the fabric of her dress as my fingers closed around the cold metal. That was as intimate as we got.

"You shouldn't be doing this," I said once I had the .38 in my hands. "You know that. You do, right?"

She turned to face me in the dark. I could smell the perfume she'd worn earlier that day, light now as it began to fade. And I could smell the booze, the red wine that'd either given her courage or brought reason to her troubled mind. It was hard to say which.

And though she was hidden from me by shadow, I could picture the face as I'd seen it before, so clean and fresh, her brunette bob too short to frame her cheeks and jaw the way they needed to be framed, leaving the youthfulness captured there stark and far from alluring. Just tired, and lost.

Chapter Two

"Something is wrong with my husband, Denton. There has to be."

That'd been only a few days ago, when she'd first come to hire me. I was fresh back from a pair of catastrophes – one upstate, the other in Arizona -- and I needed the work. Otherwise, I'd have taken a week off. My face was a mess of cuts and bruises. The goose egg I'd received from being slammed headfirst into a wall at least had gone down, but my arm was still in a sling, the shoulder dislocated three days before courtesy of my efforts to stop gunmen from turning my client into a sieve. I was run ragged, and tired. She'd looked tired then, too, at the end of her rope with something I took to mean gambling, booze, or women.

You can say a phrase twenty different ways without a struggle, using subtle differences in tone and inflection. A change of emphasis changes the meaning. I should have been paying attention to how she'd said it that first day, but my head had been elsewhere. It was still on the Mort Peters case and what had gone down at Herbie's Diner. And, if for some reason that slipped my mind, there was the Eisen Brothers fiasco, the one that had gotten me the shoulder, to give me fits when I thought of how close we'd come to botching that, as well. Suffice to say, I was distracted, and so I'd listened to the words and took my retainer, flying on autopilot, same as I would on any other case when a spouse comes in, wanting me to play spy for a few days and see if there was a reason for the doubts they were feeling.

In Sally Burgess' case, it should have been a happy ending. Earlier today, I'd given her my report in person.

"There's nothing," I'd said. "Your husband, Denton Burgess, is about as clean and regular a guy as they come. He goes to work, does his job, and he's home in the afternoon. Doesn't even stop in for a beer with the boys. Foreman says he works hard, yet he doesn't do much to draw attention. He clocks out for lunch, is always back with a few minutes to spare, and then he's back to the grindstone for the rest of his day. No tickets, no hidden bank accounts, no booze, no dope. No mistresses, far as I can tell. He attends church on Sundays, has done jury duty twice in the past three years. He votes a straight ticket in every election. No jacket with the police. No youthful indiscretions to be ashamed of. As far as I can tell, he didn't even steal an apple off the bin outside the corner store to share with his pals. Payroll has him sending a fin to his mother in Lodi every two weeks. Every other penny of it goes into the joint account the two of you share.

"There's simply nothing there that I can see, Mrs. Burgess."

She'd taken the news like I'd offered her a lunch of cold poison.

"There's something wrong with him. There has to be."

"Nothing that I can see," I'd said again, but decided to play Devil's Advocate. "He ever threaten you?"

"No."

"Get violent? Strike you?"

"No. Of course not."

"You get the feeling like he's lying to you?"

"No."

"Then congratulations are in order. Your husband isn't stepping out on you, and there's nothing in his behavior that says something untoward. You're lucky, Mrs. Burgess. I don't get to say that too often to ladies who sit where you are."

But she hadn't looked lucky, nor like she'd wanted my congratulations. She'd looked like a woman deep at the bottom of a well dug out by despair.

That was when the nagging feeling had started, and it hadn't gotten any better as the day wore on. Marisol had the afternoon off, something to do with her children, she'd said. I was alone in the office, with nothing to do but let the feeling chew on me, long after my client had paid her bill and left.

Finally, when I couldn't take it any longer, I'd driven over to the Burgesses' rented one-bedroom above the flower shop where Sally would occasionally fill in. The factory where Denton worked hummed twenty-four hours a day. He'd recently pulled a stint on the mid-shift and wouldn't be home until after ten sometime. I'd arrived at nine-fifty, creeping up the steps and entering the home without knocking, almost sure of what I'd find and not liking it much when I did.

"Where does Denton keep this?" I asked, meaning the piece. "We can't have him knowing about it. You know we can't."

"Why not?" she asked.

"Because you don't give a guy a shock like that when he gets home from work."

"He needs to know," was all she said.

"Why?"

She made a face to say the answer was

obvious. "Because I shouldn't be the only one who does."

Chapter Three

"You're not. I know."

But of course, that wasn't enough, and I knew it the moment the words left my mouth. Better that I'd said nothing at all.

"Denton's a swell guy. Knowing you were playing around with something that's supposed to keep you safe would only worry him. You don't want that, do you?"

I could feel her eyes close and heard the sigh build from six feet deep in her chest.

"Sock drawer. Bedroom," she said. "Make sure you cover it up with the unmentionables and that you keep it all neat. Denton notices things like that. He was in the Navy."

In the bedroom, I replaced the pistol and arranged the scene like a military man would expect it. The differences in the Army and Navy were wide and clear, and any man who'd served in either branch would be happy to tell you all about it if you made the mistake of bringing it up. But stowing your drawers? There weren't too many different ways to do that, and so I could be reasonably sure he would never notice.

"How'd you know it was me and not Denton when I arrived?" I asked as I slid the drawer closed.

"How do you know I could tell the difference?"

"Because I came in without knocking, and you didn't immediately give me the business."

There was another deep sigh, partly of frustration with me, and partly because of something else. But, to her credit, she answered.

"Denton has a peculiar way of taking the stairs. He says it's something to do with the rolling deck on a ship. Whatever it is, I've heard it what feels like a million times now. I could pick his walk out of a million. When I heard you coming up, I knew it wasn't him from the moment your feet first hit the base board."

Sally was sitting when I returned. She'd switched from red wine to gin and was gripping her glass with a pair of shaky hands and taking big swallows. She offered me one in a voice tinier than the hiccup of an apartment in which she lived, but I declined. I was never here, as far as I was concerned.

The trip to the bedroom was only a few steps there, a few steps back again. The apartment wasn't any bigger than mine, though with two people living in it, it must have felt tiny and cramped. Days where you were home and with nothing to do, you'd get right on top of each other all day, nowhere to go. A brief part of me wondered if that'd been why she'd come to me, but the smarter part of me knew it

wasn't, straight off. It was something else.
Something far more bizarre to the conventional
mind.

"So?" I asked with some added force
behind my words. She was looking dull in the
eyes, and I figured she needed an ounce or two
of the rough to shake her out of it. The trick
worked perfectly, and her face cleared up
considerably between another gulp of the gin
and when her eyes turned upwards toward me,
like she was just noticing I was there.

"You know how it is," she replied.

"I know how it is most of the time, sure,
but not here. Give it to me straight. What's got
you so convinced there's something queer
about your husband?"

She shook her head. "I don't know. Maybe
I'm wrong. Sure, I am. That's what you're going
to say, isn't it?"

"I already did. Earlier today. You don't
need to hear it again."

"Maybe I did. Maybe I still do."

We could have gone round and round on it.
She had her defenses up now in spite of the
booze. She was playing it stupid, or coy,
anything to keep me from getting answers. I
needed to figure what buttons to push, but, just
then, a shoed foot hit the bottom of the stairs in
a way that made her jump. And just like that
our little game became a moot point. It was
Denton, home a little earlier than I'd expected.

"He's coming," she whispered.

Yeah, but it was slow going. I understood then what she meant by his peculiar walk. The man I'd followed didn't betray anything of the like, but it was clear some injury affected his ability to climb a flight of stairs. It wasn't just the step a of an ex-Navy man, then.

I put a finger across my lips and nodded towards the coat closet just to the side of the kitchen doorway. She gave the nod, and I slipped inside, closing it behind me. Everything hanging within gave a sway at my intrusion.

Chapter Four

The front door opened, and I heard Denton Burgess speak for the first time. It was a calm voice, not unkind. It was like most I'd heard, in fact, just like his face was like most you saw. He wasn't much, especially in comparison to his wife, who, even when she looked as haggard as I'd seen her, was stunning enough she could kill you twice and revive you once.

"Well, good evening," he said, surprise in his voice, but not much else.

It's an eternal mystery to me how a plain-faced guy could ever tire of a beautiful woman, especially when he knew he was marrying up. But this wasn't a man grown weary of his wife, so I didn't have to wonder on that score. It was just that he was so, well, normal. Nothing he did was surprising. If I had a girl like that at home, waiting for me, coming home every day would be like a birthday party full of balloons and noise makers. A normal guy like Denton didn't think anything of it. He was just so average, he couldn't even conceive of something beyond his ken. He'd probably never thought twice of why a staggering beauty had ever agreed to settle down with him. He'd probably just assumed that was the way it was, all over the world.

"Good evening, darling. How was your day?" she asked, her tone changed to something welcoming, if not gushing.

"Lousy. I'm beat. What are you still doing up?"

"I couldn't sleep. Thought a night cap might help."

"Sure, it will. It'll have you snoring away in no time."

"Don't tease. I don't snore, do I?"

"Like a Harley."

"No!"

Denton laughed, and I could hear the smack of lips when they broke their embrace.

"You drinking it neat tonight, honey?" he asked. "I could get tight just off your kiss."

"Well, if I want it to do what I want it to do, it doesn't make much sense to water it down, does it?"

"Now that you mention it."

"I have dinner for you in the oven. Do you

want something to eat before--?"

"Nah. I'm beat, I said. I'll eat when I've grabbed a few hours."

"No! Don't bother hanging up your coat."

I tensed, expecting then for the closet door to open and leave me face-to-face with a guy who would jump to conclusions. But Sally was too quick for that.

"Just throw it over the chair, there. I'll hang it up later."

"Why don't you come to bed with me?" he asked.

"I'd really rather not tonight, Denton. I'm sorry."

"Not what I'm talking about. Maybe if I'm next to you, it'll help you sleep."

"I...sure, Denton. Sure."

There was a clatter of his lunch pail settling onto the floor, and the thumps of his boots as he pulled them off and set them near the front door.

"Say, throw open the bedroom window, would you?" Denton said. "It's stuffy in here. I need to breathe."

They went to bed after that, no other words between them. What they had said had held the timbre of a dialogue spoken in some variation a thousand times. I let out a long breath I'd been holding since what felt like his arrival. A distant click of a lamp switch was the last I heard of them. Afterwards time slowed down to a crawl. I was left standing ramrod straight in the closet, which got stuffy with my hot breath within minutes. My only company was the occasional tickle of a coat or other object brushing against my back. Every time it happened felt like the first time, and every time I tried not to jump or otherwise give myself away to Denton Burgess.

The dark was there, too, and it seemed to devour not just all the light but time itself. It felt like two or three hours before I could hear snoring. It wasn't Sally's, either. It was coming from a masculine throat, and boy, was it tearing down the wallpaper.

I let it go on a while, just long enough I knew Denton Burgess was out and not coming back until the roosters were crowing. The bedroom was straight across from the closet as I exited, and I could see Sally lying on her back in bed. Denton was on his stomach, one long arm hanging over the side of the bed until it nearly touched the floor. His face was half buried in a pillow, and his mouth was wide open. Sally was staring right at me, peering over her husband's back with big, dark eyes that I only knew were there because of the way some far-off street light made them shine.

She said nothing, just watched me go out the front door without so much as a whisper, pull it closed, and tiptoe down the stairs.

Chapter Five

I went straight home to bed and was back up again by five, arriving at the office by seven. The sun was up, and it was looking like another scorcher of a day. Benny, who owned the newsstand across the street from my office, was quick to tell me the Angels had won the day before. I bought a paper and grabbed three detective magazines off the rack. Black Mask, Thrilling Dime Detective, and one I hadn't seen before, Astonishing Oriental Mysteries.

"A real barn burner," he said, presumably of the baseball game. I shrugged and plunked down enough to cover costs and a little extra. Benny was putting his oldest through trade school and needed it where he could get it. I had it, and so he got it.

"Y'know, Hardwood, I don't get you," he said. Like any good news agent, he was fat and jowly. His skin always looked like a sausage casing with too much meat stuffed into it.

"What's not to get?" I asked.

"Here you are, you got your own agency. You're doing your own cases. It's the real stuff, yet you come in every week and buy these rags from me. The sleazier, the better with you, too."

"I'm new to the game," I replied. "Consider these instruction manuals."

Benny roared way louder than the quip called for, but that wasn't unusual. He was one of those guys who lived life just a little more joyously than the average gee, and everything that came out of him was just a little bigger as a result.

I took my parcel and left. The resident dentist was just coming around the corner as I approached the building where our offices were located. He nodded at me and looked like he wanted to play nice. About a month ago, he'd sold out one of my Hollywood clients to a gossip columnist, a harpy named Agatha Tate. It'd cost me the client, and I'd nearly throttled him for it. I would have spit in his eye, but I'd been told by building management to be a good boy, so that's how I played it.

"Hopkins," I said. "How's tricks?"

"Hello, Hardwood. Angels won yesterday. Did you hear?"

"Apparently it's all anyone can talk about. Hey, I was thinking you should open a candy store down the block, catch 'em coming and going."

"Funny. Never heard that one before."

"What? I'm calling Schenectady. They said that joke was certified fresh."

We pushed inside. Our landlady, Joy Kefalas, was dusting the lobby's sparse furnishings. She saw me and nodded to the coffee table in the center of the room, where something wrapped in aluminum lay.

"Sfakianopita," she said. "Dr. Hopkins. How're you today?"

"Swell, Mrs. Kefalas. Say, why are you feeding him and not me?"

"Because you have a beautiful wife to do all of that for you, and he doesn't," she replied. To me, she added, "Dunk that in some coffee. You'll love it."

"I love anything that I don't have to cook," I replied and took up my care package without missing a step.

"You cook?" Hopkins asked. He made it sound like I did it while wearing a tutu.

"If you call it that. I make a mean breakfast and a corned beef hash so ugly, its own mother won't claim it."

Upstairs, my secretary let me know I had a busy day. Busy for me, anyway. An hour later, I was two clients deep in my waiting area, with my old friend and client, Ann Spurlock, talking my ear off.

"Judy Pena still swears by you, by the way," she said to me. We'd met through Judy, and when Ann had come along with a story about how her husband, Michael, was stepping out on her, I'd taken her on. "You helped find her Ricky when he went missing last year."

"How is Mrs. Pena?" I asked. I was trying not to be distracted, but last night had me worried still. I felt like I'd reset the timer on a bomb without defusing it.

"Fine. Ricky...well..."

"Some souls are just lost, Ann," I said. "They come into this world that way, and it doesn't change until they go out again. Most of them earlier than they should."

"But that's not my Michael," she insisted.

"That's certainly not what I'm implying, and pardon me if it came off as such. In fact, unless something has changed, your husband is clean as a whistle."

A lot of that going around, lately.

"I'm not so sure about that."

A lot of that, too.

"With all due respect, Ann, you weren't sure the last time you came in to hire me, but I didn't find anything, then, either."

"Yes, and you told me to get lost unless I found something else about him."

"I wouldn't put it in those words, but yes, I concluded our business arrangement. It isn't ethical to keep taking money from a woman for nothing. Now, do you have new information you can share?"

She pulled a rueful face that made me take notice. "I'd say."

"What?"

"Michael's been leaving town lately, going off to spend nights in a hotel."

"No reason why?"

She shrugged. "He says it's for work, but

that makes no sense. Why would he need to leave town if he works in the planning office?"

I chewed my lip. "Okay, that is something."

Her face brightened. "So, you believe me?"

"I believe that he's leaving town and staying in motels if you say he is. It doesn't prove anything, of course, but I can look into it for you, if you like."

"I do. I'm telling you, Johnny, there's something wrong. There has to be!"

The phrasing hit me like it was made out of fists. Something must have shown on my face, as Ann Spurlock gave me a look.

"You all right?"

"Yeah. Fine. Look, Ann, I'll take you on again as a client, but only on one condition."

She lifted her chin. "Such as?" she asked.

"You have to agree that, whatever I find or don't find, you accept my report as is."

"Well, I just don't see what—"

"Ma'am, I say this not because I might find something. You've said as much that you think I will. But, should I find out your husband is still clean, you have to agree to accept that and drop the whole business."

"But you—"

"Those are my conditions."

She didn't like it, but I got a big smile from her anyway. "Fair enough. I know you'll do a good job, Johnny. You're very good to me, you know."

Chapter Six

Ann Spurlock left cash to retain my services and swept out, sunny as a day in May. Would that every client could be like her. It felt criminal, taking her money like this, but I had to say, this new twist was an interesting one. It certainly looked as if Michael Spurlock was every bit the cad his wife was starting to believe he was.

The other two cases, while not as intriguing, had enough meat to interest me. I took each. By noon, I had more work than I could handle: a background check on a teaching candidate at a private, all-boys school, a dodgy insurance claim, and Ann Spurlock's potentially wayward husband. I got the impression none of them were going to be happy with my findings, but they didn't have to, so long as the checks cleared. What I needed, as I stood at the office's front door watching the insurance guy disappear down the stairwell, was a little tea and sympathy. What I got instead was Marisol Gutierrez.

"Mr. Levine," she said. She'd been paid recently, and so her English was almost

114

pristine. "He say call him."

"Concerning?"

"Mort Peters."

I sighed. "He's still dead, unless I missed something."

"There are problems."

"That case was nothing but. Do you have an effervescent on you?"

She nodded and produced a small, solemnly decorated foil packet, but I had to fetch my own water from the drinking fountain across the hall. The water cooler guy didn't swing by until day after tomorrow.

I dosed myself and went back to my office, where I stared at the wall instead of doing my job. When that didn't satisfy, I picked up the paper and scanned the headlines, front to back. Of course, there wouldn't be anything there. By the time I'd left the Burgess' apartment, it was nearly eleven o'clock, far past time when the morning edition would be put to bed. I looked anyway.

Marisol knocked on the office door and wanted to know where we were going to start. It'd been a while since we'd had more than one client at a time, and she was as excited as she was capable of being, which is to say there was almost a twinkle in her dead-eyed stare.

"The teacher's the easiest," I replied. "We've got his work history in the file the school left us. Start running that down and see if anything funny pops up: discrepancies in

dates, gaps in employment, the like. And make
sure to confirm with his old bosses he left for
the reasons he gave. Call, don't write, but see if
they can mail us whatever they have. After that,
check with the police departments in the places
where he lived. See if anyone has a file on him.
I'll check in with Stashe at police headquarters
to see if there's anything local, and then I'll do
the same with the LA County Sheriff's
Department. I can look up the insurance
claimant while I'm there, kill two birds with
one stone."

"Are you leaving now?" she asked.

I told her I was, and not to expect me for
the rest of the afternoon. After all of that I
would take a ride over to City Hall, since I'd be
halfway there once I was done at the sheriff's
department. Maybe they'd have a practical
reason for why Michael Spurlock was going out
of town so often.

City Hall was convenient because the
flower shop was on the way. Traffic was light,
and I was able to tool my powder blue Chevy
into a space across the street so I could peer
through the plate glass windows at what was
going on inside. Sally Burgess was picking up a
shift that day. She wore a blue and white flower
print dress that was too on the nose for the
work she was doing. Her face bore a smile, but
the eyes were as tired and haunted as I'd seen
them the night before. No one paid them any
attention, nor did the customers appear to ask

how she was doing.

They didn't care. It was a funny thing we did, believing that customers in flower shops actually cared about their fellow man. That's why they were buying flowers in the first place, their actions said. But it wasn't the case, nor would it ever be. A person coming at you with a bouquet of flowers was carrying a dead thing, a tightly bound batch of corpses held together with a rubber band or a piece of string. It didn't get any more desperate and oblivious than that. The look in Sally Burgess' eyes said she was the only flower shop girl in the world who saw the irony for what it was.

Chapter Seven

The morning was busy for her, but I was determined to wait until everyone had cleared out. I needed to know now before I went anywhere else. Usually, I could juggle more than one thing in my head at a time, work more than one angle to get done what needed doing. Today, I couldn't. I'd been met the night before with something I knew without knowing, yet it remained inexplicable to me at the same time. I had to find answers before I could do anything else.

The problem was, I didn't know any of the questions.

She took a break about ten a.m. The shop had cleared out of little old ladies and guilty husbands who'd forgotten an important date. I watched her pour a cup of something hot from a Thermos she kept under the counter, taking the drink and a cigarette outside to the bottom step of the staircase up to their apartment, where she sat.

I kept out of her sight as I crossed the street. I didn't know how she'd react to seeing me again, but I didn't want to spook her.

I needn't have bothered. She smiled a little when she saw me round the corner. It wasn't a happy smile, nor was it particularly warm. It was like her face was doing what it knew it was supposed to do.

"Good morning," she said.

"Good morning," I replied. "How are you feeling today?"

"Better, thank you." She smoked and eyed me. "I must have given you a terrible fright last night."

"For a moment." I took out a cigarette, and she passed me her matchbook. It was midnight blue and bore a name in swirling gold script. When I was satisfied with my light, I passed it back to her. "The Regal," I said. "Never heard of it."

"It's a club," she said. "I worked there as a cigarette girl before I met my husband."

"Did you meet there?" She shook her head. "That matchbook is new. Did you go dancing there recently?"

Again, she shook her head. "We don't go dancing. We don't go anywhere, really. We just do our same little thing, every day. That's our life together, Mr. Hardwood."

I grunted, preferring to smoke instead of answering out loud.

"You don't seem all that surprised. You must already know what all of this is."

I shrugged. "Could be that I know, could be not," I said. "The smart play is always to keep what you think you know to yourself until you're sure of it. After that, you can be smug and strut around like you have all the answers."

"Sounds like good advice. So, why are you here? Is it really to check up on me? Because I'm fine, now. It was just a moment, but that's over with."

"Is it?"

"You don't sound convinced. So, I guess that's the real reason for your visit. And here I was, thinking that I had a handsome man calling after my own health and well-being."

"I am. After a fashion."

"And what fashion is that?"

"You stay healthy so long as your husband does. If he should go some other direction, and you're to blame, they'll walk you straight into the death house. You have to know it."

"Assuming they know who did it."

"Mrs. Burgess, when I found you last night, you were standing in the middle of your

apartment with your husband's loaded gun in
your hands. Say I hadn't come along, and
events had gone the way they looked like they
would. No, don't. Don't sing me any songs
about your innocence. It's just a hypothetical.
You can stand a hypothetical, can't you? Well,
so what of it? Do you think you could have
somehow avoided the cops noticing that you'd
had something to do with your husband's
death? It's just that, from what I've seen, you
lack the kind of cunning it takes to kill a man
and get away with it."

"You don't know what I'm capable of."

"Oh, I've a decent idea," I said. I let the rest
of that thought hang unspoken on the air.

She finished her cigarette and started
nursing her tea. She held it in both hands,
trying to look like a little girl who needed both
to keep a decent grip on the cup. Or, she was
trying to appear cold, even though the morning
was already eighty degrees and climbing.

"Are you going to report me to the police,
Mr. Hardwood?"

I made a non-committal noise in my throat.

"What do I have to do to convince you I'm
not a threat?" she asked.

"Nothing radical. Just don't do anything
rash, and over time, I'll stop coming around to
check up on you."

"So, that's what you plan to do, is it? Come
around often?"

"Until I'm satisfied."

"And what if I just wait you out and then do the deed?"

I took the cigarette from my mouth and considered the smoldering end of it. It'd burnt down so it looked like it had a point.

"You're not that cold-blooded, Mrs. Burgess, whatever you'll have me believe. Anything you do, it'll be in the moment. So, if it's going to happen, it'll happen soon. You certainly won't be able to wait me out."

"I wouldn't bet on that."

"I'm not worried. Listen, tell me something."

"Sure."

"Why do you stay? I know you're bored."

"I'm not bored," she replied. "I'm horrified."

Chapter Eight

I gave her the look that said her answer had better be a good one as I asked, "At what?"

"At him." She sipped her tea and considered the murky brown in the cup much as I had my cigarette. I wondered what she saw there, if anything. "I married him because I wanted comfort. Security. Every girl wants that, right?"

"I know a few who don't, but sure. Most do."

"Well, I wish I could be one of those kinds of women, taking my fun where I can find it. But that's not me. I'm not that woman. Denton's good-looking, and he has a good job. It's not much, but it keeps us fed and in this place." She threw her head back and looked all around, eyes not focusing on anything. She'd already seen everything there was to see of the place a thousand times over.

"Sounds like the basis for most marriages," I said. "At least, from the ones I've seen."

"You've never been married, then?"

"Not even close."

"Well, part of it is getting to the truth. Do you know what I mean? How many lies do you tell on a date?"

"Not half as many as a woman tells, but plenty."

"And why do that?"

I shrugged.

"You don't want to say it, do you?" she asked.

"Does anybody?"

She smiled then. It was genuine, but a genuine show of teeth, really. It was hard to figure her. She sounded normal one minute, and the next she was looking like she needed to be in a padded cell. But I got the impression she had the game between men and women figured, and she didn't disappoint.

"And you know how hard it would be to tell the truth. When you go out with someone, you tell them a version of you so they don't run screaming in the other direction. You talk about an idealized version of who you could be, or maybe who you want to be. It's only after you get married that two people start to learn the truth of each other. It's fun. It's like solving a crossword puzzle in the newspaper. You have clues, but those clues can mean two or three different things. It's up to you to figure out what they are and try to make the answer fit in the boxes you're given.

"It takes years. I don't know, decades, even. I see these old people walking up and down the streets, still holding hands. Or not. There's an old man who comes into the shop. Mr. Sue, we call him. His name isn't Sue like a lady's name. He's from Korea, barely speaks any English, but he speaks enough that he orders petunias for his wife when we have them. She's also from Korea, but when they moved here, she fell in love with vases full of flowers. She wants cut flowers just like the American women get here, he says.

"When they met, he probably didn't know this about her. He had to find it out. Maybe it took years to learn it, but now that he knows it, it's become part of their routine. You know? He goes out, he buys her flowers."

"Denton doesn't buy you flowers?" I asked.

"That's not the point. Come on, Mr. Hardwood, you came here to get answers, and I'm giving them to you. And you're smarter than this. It's why I hired you."

I decided to cut the baloney and give it to her straight. "Okay, I'm gonna assume that your husband isn't all that complicated."

She had a mouthful of tea when I said this. She snorted through her nose and swallowed with a single, painful gulp.

"That's an understatement. Mr. Hardwood, as impossible as it may sound, Denton didn't lie a single time to me on any date we ever went on. Not only didn't he lie, but by the time we were married, I knew everything there was to know about him. Everything."

"And so there was nothing for you to learn over the years. But how do you know that? It could be that he has one or two surprises up his sleeve for you."

She shook her head. "No, he doesn't. I know everything already. I know his favorite color, his favorite baseball team, what he likes for dinner, who he votes for in elections. I even know about a time he went whitewater rafting with his uncles in Missouri and nearly drowned. Everything. There is nothing he can say or do that I don't predict before it happens because there is nothing new to report. It never occurs to him to do it differently, either, and every time I've tried to get him to change up his routine, he just smiles and keeps doing what he's doing. He won't listen."

She looked down into her lap at the cup. There was a sip left, and she drained it. Break time was over, I guessed.

"That's what I'm terrified of, Mr. Hardwood. I'm terrified that this is all there's ever going to be. Do you know what that can do to someone? To know everything about another person that quickly? To never get the adventure everyone else gets, of discovering the real person beneath the skin of the man they married? It gets to me sometimes, and I occasionally do crazy things as a result. I'm sorry I dragged you into one of those episodes."

She tried to go around me, but I stopped her with a hand on her arm. "Why don't you just leave, then?" I asked.

I already knew the answer to that, too, but I asked it anyway, and she answered it because it was the thing to do.

"Because it's like you said, Mr. Hardwood, there's a lot to like. I know how lucky I am. I'm not a fool. The next one might not be as nice, or as hard-working. Or worse."

She was halfway around the corner when I called out, "You'll think of something, Mrs. Burgess. I know you will."

She paused a moment, as if in thought, and then continued on her way.

Chapter Nine

Weeks passed. I drove by the flower shop a

few times in that span, but Mrs. Burgess was never there when I would come by. Once, I went up to their apartment just to see if the name was still on the mailbox. It made me wonder if she were doing this purposely, keeping out of my sight. Of course, that was a silly notion. People were interesting to me, but I've never been all that interesting to other people. That is to say, they stay in my memory far longer than I stay in theirs.

In the meantime, I worked my other cases. The insurance claim held water, and Michael Spurlock continued to appear like a decent man. The schoolteacher, though, was the real prize. He certainly turned out to be far less clean than Denton Burgess. I wound up taking a ride on the Big Chief from LA to Chicago to talk to a little private school there, run by a group of former Jesuits. The teacher had been let go because of rumors of a relationship with one of the students. They wouldn't elaborate, but they didn't have to. This was the sort of thing my employers would want to hear, and they rightfully refused the man a job.

I paid him a visit a few days later to say he needed to try a new line of work. He got sore enough to take a poke at me, but he was apparently better around little boys than he was real men. To my credit, I didn't give him anything in return except a swift kick in the pants when he overbalanced throwing his haymaker. That sent him into a trash can outside the boarding house where he was staying. The racket roused the widow who ran the joint. I told her what I'd found, as well, just in case she wanted to know the kind of gee she was offering room and board. She thanked me and let the man know he had until sundown to pack his things and get out. A job well done, in my opinion.

More cases came and went, but every day before setting out to beat the pavement I would scan through the papers, looking for what I was sure would be the next time Mrs. Burgess would have one of her episodes, as she called them. More than once I considered calling the police about her, but I knew they'd laugh me out of the joint if I told them there was a woman somewhere in LA who was maybe perhaps sort of thinking of killing her husband. "Her and every other wife," they'd undoubtedly tell me, pat me on the head, and give me an all-day sucker for my troubles.

A month later I found what I'd been looking for. I'd mostly paid interest to the crime beat, expecting to see something about a domestic call ending in a murder. But it was actually on page three where I found a little article about an altercation at a nightclub. A name jumped out at me. The altercation had taken place at The Regal. I read further, and there was another name: Denton Burgess.

He and his wife were having a night on the town for her birthday when a man who worked at the club, named Ed Sparks, started chatting up Burgess' wife, a woman incorrectly identified in the story as Lola. Little mention was made of Denton doing anything about this until "Lola", apparently unhappy with a man making time with her in front of her husband, gave Sparks the slap. Sparks then roughed her up a little -- nothing much.

It was at this point Denton Burgess stepped in and pummeled Sparks until several patrons pulled him off. No arrests were made, and the club's owner, a man named Dooley, apologized to the couple for his employee's bad behavior.

I asked around at the police station. No one had pressed charges on either side, so I dug a little further. Something about the whole thing bugged me. I knew what I knew without knowing it, and that was always the worst feeling. I'm the kind of man who can't stand incomplete things. Tie the threads together, paint in what is missing, patch up the holes. It'd been an obsession of mine since I was a kid. When others were telling me to leave something alone, I just couldn't.

So, I made reservations that evening for The Regal. It was a pleasant enough joint. If you've been to a supper club with pretensions towards being great but falling instead into being just good enough that you'd come back a second or even third time, you've been there. I don't need to describe it to you. They're mostly the same.

They seated me near the back of the room,
which was fine. I had a tomato bisque to start.
The pork roast was good, but a little heavy on
the garlic, and the potatoes were slathered in
herbs and butter. The single malt I ordered as a
chaser was a little too austere for my tastes,
and so I switched to coffee.

It was the third night of a week-long
engagement by some Borscht Belt comedian
whose name I forgot immediately and decided
to call Schlomo Yutz instead. It was a gas, that
name. Somebody had to make me laugh, and it
certainly wasn't this guy. The rest of the crowd
was a little more polite.

Management was smart. Schlomo did
thirty minutes, a warm-up for their house band,
a quartet called The Regalites. According to a
couple sitting at the next table, they were the
real draw in the place. That, and dessert. That
was good because their taste in humor stank to
high Heaven.

While the band played, I spotted a couple
of gees parked near my table. They were
dressed well, hair perfect, and they watched
everything with the easy smugness of men who
were in control.

There were two, a big redhead with a
cauliflower ear, and a smaller one, a dusky-
skinned Sicilian, who I took to be the brains of
the duo because he didn't look like he'd been
beaten half to death on the regular. It was him I
spoke to.

129

"Sparks not in tonight?" I asked.

"Who's asking?" the smaller man said. And by "smaller", I mean that he was about my height. The redhead had roughly six inches and sixty pounds on us both. It made me wonder what savages there were lurking around that had given him the ear. It was enough to make you want to lock your doors at night.

"The name's Rollo. His night off?" I asked.

"What are you, one of his Army buddies?"

"Something like that."

The guy gave a knowing smile. "Lotta you running around," he replied. "I think Eddie must'a fought more engagements in the war than that draft dodger, John Wayne."

"His pals show up often? Maybe I know a few."

"I doubt it. But yeah, they're in here all the time. He's a popular kid."

"Say, I think I read in the paper someone really slapped him around some. That one of his Army buddies?"

"That?" The Sicilian laughed. "Dinner and a show. We aim to please."

I stuck around to listen to The Regalites. They really were worth the ticket. Afterward, I drove over to the Little Doggie Bar for a night cap. There were no cases lined up, so I indulged myself just enough that I had to walk the two blocks home.

Chapter Ten

The next day, I drove over to the flower shop. She wasn't in, however. The owner, a woman in her mid-fifties by the look of her, greeted me instead.

"She's taken ill," she said.

"Has she?" I asked. "Well, I'm a friend of the family. I'll just pop upstairs to see if she's all right."

"Oh, you really shouldn't." It wasn't a pleasant warning. Were she a man, there would have been intent to physically stop me, if necessary.

"Why is that?" I asked.

"She's under the weather, and you wouldn't want to catch whatever she's got."

"Oh, I've probably had it a time or two myself. I grew up in a rough neighborhood."

I left before the confusion had fully passed over her face, turning right just outside and in through the doorway that led up to the apartment. When I knocked on the door, it took a minute for Mrs. Burgess to answer. She kept the door closed between us.

"It's Johnny Hardwood, Mrs. Burgess." I

had to raise my voice a little to be heard.

"Go away. I'm not feeling well."

"So I've been told."

"What are you even doing here? I'm no longer your client."

"No, you're not. I'm just checking up on you. It's part of the service I provide."

"I seriously doubt that. Please go away."

"I read about you in the papers yesterday."

"So?"

"Is your husband in?"

"No."

"How about you let me in so we can talk?"

"I assure you, Mr. Hardwood, we have nothing to talk about."

"Okay, we can do it here if you like. I know about Ed Sparks. I remember the new matchbook from The Regal. I know you saw Ed Sparks before your birthday party, and I know Ed is one of those guys who's willing to do a lot of things for money. Including maybe pretend to come on to you so you could slap him across the mouth. It couldn't have been too hard for him to take the job. A little scratch in his pocket, a beautiful woman to manhandle. You made it easy for him."

The pause afterward was just dramatic enough you could have used it in a film, then the door opened a little. I saw a sliver of Mrs. Burgess' face, eyeing me through the crack. She said nothing, an offer that I should continue.

"May I come in?" I asked.

"Why are you here?" was her reply.

"The same reason as the last time I visited, to make sure you and your husband are all right."

"You should just go."

"Five minutes, and I will. Deal?"

She rolled her eyes the way women do when they're tired of arguing and threw open the door, standing there where I could see everything. She was dressed in a housecoat and slippers, the way someone sick would dress. Her brown hair was a mess, and she wore no makeup.

Normally I would say that even as sloppily dressed as she was, she was still beautiful, but at the moment, her face was no picnic. The right side, the side she'd hidden from me when peeking out through the crack in the door, was swollen and black around the eye. The bruise was large enough that it wasn't a punch. It couldn't have come from anything less than a slap with some elbow grease on it, maybe even a backhand that got the knuckles involved.

I stepped inside, removing my hat as I went.

"I'd offer you a cold drink," she said, "but since you'll only be five minutes..."

Clever.

"How'd you get the eye?" I asked. That was underselling it. It was worst around the eye, but the bruise took up half of her face. "Sparks didn't give you that."

133

"No, he didn't. How'd you find out?"

"From the papers."

"You know what I mean."

She turned on her heel, and I followed over to what passed for the living room. We sat, and she started to smoke. I was feeling all right at the moment, no itch to light up, and so instead I laid it out for her.

"It wasn't hard to put it all together. I've been keeping an eye out. I half-expected to see one of you in the obituary column."

She let fly with a cloud of smoke from the bottom of her lungs. "Don't be so melodramatic, Mr. Hardwood. It was never like that."

"So you keep saying. But it was enough that you started thinking that you had to do something. Which reminds me. The Regal. You started going there before you hired me. That was why you had the matchbook when I saw you that last time. Why?"

She shrugged. "My uncle owns it, you know."

"No, I didn't. That doesn't answer my question."

She shrugged. "I don't know. I just needed a few kicks, I suppose."

"You went there to see the old gang, have a drink or two. Feel alive."

"Yes. And there's no harm in that!"

"Of course not. And maybe that's what it was, at first. But you went back, maybe more than once, and who you spent time with got real specific. You can't expect me to believe it was innocent, after that."

"I don't care what you believe, Mr. Hardwood."

"Good. So you won't mind if I speculate, then."

"The sands in the hourglass are running. Have your fun."

"What was it, huh? An affair? Did you go there looking for someone to try it on with? Eventually, it must have crossed your mind. But it's like you said. You aren't going to leave your husband. There's always the fear you'll be trading down, is that it?

"But then you remember Ed Sparks. Oh, he's a character, isn't he? A big guy, I'd imagine. Tough. A bouncer, but he's willing to do a lot of things in exchange for money. Roll a drunk, beat up a husband with a wandering eye. He might even be willing to help you with a little project you had in mind. You've got to have something, right? Something to get your heart racing a little. You've been squirreling some money away for a while. That's how you hired me without your husband knowing how you were spending his hard-earned pay. I'd wager you have a second account, and if I tossed this place I'd find that account book hidden somewhere nice and safe, like the pantry. Or under the mattress in your bedroom."

"You wouldn't dare!"

I shook my head. "I don't need answers

that badly. But I'm right aren't I? About the account?"

"Yes." She didn't even bother to pretend being ashamed about it. "It was my father's. He passed earlier this year. I've been putting a little of what I make at the flower shop in there."

"Did it buy you what you wanted, or did you originally ask Ed to do something else for you, like bump off Denton after work? You know exactly when he'll be home every night, even if he's going to be late. Ed could be waiting for him one night with a knife or a length of piano wire. It gets dark out there, on the landing outside your apartment, and there's no one around after business hours."

"That's ridiculous."

"Is it?"

"If I wanted him dead, you know I could have done it myself. That's what had you so upset, wasn't it? Besides, my money bought me exactly what I wanted."

"Did it?"

She looked away in a pout.

"You wanted Ed to pretend to hit on you so your husband would get jealous."

She shrugged.

"What's the rest of it?"

She didn't say anything else, so I kept on speculating. "If Denton didn't show enough sand, maybe you'd let Ed go further? Eventually? A big, strong guy, treating you just like you deserve, and then you'd let slip to your husband in an oh-so-clever way that you'd been stepping out. What kind of reaction would you have expected then, I wonder?"

"You've got a lot of theories."

"You're not an easy case, Mrs. Burgess. Your motives have seemed simple, yet I can't quite understand them."

"Well, let me put your mind at ease. Eddie's a handsome man, and I may be many things, but I'm not a killer. Nor would I hire someone to do it for me. No, I just wanted to get Denton's attention."

"So you hired Ed to do what he did."

"Yes."

"And did it go like it was supposed to?"

She frowned. "No, it didn't."

"Denton didn't take the bait."

"No, he didn't!" The words were almost a shriek of outrage. "He sat there grinning. He thought it was all a big joke, which I guess it was. And Eddie was hamming it up a little. He didn't care how he did. He was getting paid. Denton probably thought it was part of the show they did there. Uncle Felix likes bringing in comedians. It was all just a big laugh to him."

"So, you pretended to take offense to something Ed said or did so you could slap him. That wasn't originally in the script, was it?"

"No, it wasn't. Neither was Eddie getting rough with me, either. He must not have liked getting slapped by a broad like me because he really went ape over it."

Chapter Eleven

She rolled up her sleeve and showed a bruise on her arm near the elbow joint. The purplish discoloration had three pink gaps in it, delineating where Ed's fingers had grabbed her when he started to shake.

"I guess my crying out is what shook Denton loose because he jumped up all of a sudden and lit into Eddie. He was only supposed to warn him off. I know Denton. He's not a violent man. He would never have given anyone more than a warning, but he really let Eddie have it, Mr. Hardwood. But good, he did."

"Was Eddie taking it part of the act?" I asked.

Mrs. Burgess swallowed hard. "I don't think so. The money was just to get fresh, then back down when Denton wagged a finger in Eddie's face. At best maybe a sock to the jaw, you know? I just wanted him to do something that wasn't the same old Denton."

"How far did your husband go?"

"Bad enough that the other bouncer and a couple of men from nearby tables had to pull him off. I'd never seen such a look in a man's eyes before. He was speaking, saying something, but it wasn't real words. I tell you, Mr. Hardwood, it was like seeing a caveman attack Eddie. If those men hadn't pulled him off, I think Denton would have murdered him on the spot. It took a while to get him calmed down."

"And in the meantime, you had to smooth it over with your uncle, let him know the score with Eddie and all that."

She nodded. "Yes. It wasn't supposed to go that far. Uncle Felix got Denton up to his office to calm him down. They got him a drink, and he was eventually back to himself. How did you know I spoke to my uncle about it?"

"Because Eddie wouldn't still have a job if he'd done what he did, and the house hadn't been in on the maneuver."

"Ah. Yes."

"You hadn't thought of that, had you, before you hired Ed to pull that stunt?"

"Well, I always knew I could speak with my uncle about it if anything happened. He's a sweet man, really. He even got Eddie a taxi ride over to the hospital to get his face looked at when it was over. He was a mess."

"After the cops left?"

"They never came. A critic from The Times was in to see The Regalites, and he wrote about the fight instead. I guess that's how it made the papers. The police heard about it later and came to question us. We didn't press charges, and neither did Eddie, so they don't care."

I took in a deep breath and let it out slowly. Sally Burgess was at the end of her story, and I let it all sink in.

"And they all lived happily ever after," I said. I slapped my knees to put an end to it, and stood to leave, taking my fedora from the coffee table.

"Aren't you going to ask me how I got this?" she asked, showing me the bruise on her face.

"I already did, and you were like a clam about it. Anyway, I know well enough how you got it, Mrs. Burgess. Up until a day ago, your husband was just some guy. Normal. Regular habits. Affable. No dirt on him. But you couldn't stand that. You had to make him into something else, or you would go mad. So, you did just that thing. I say congratulations. You did what I couldn't do, which was find something new about him that you didn't already know.

"You know now he's got a limit. Push him past that point, and he's dangerous. I don't know if that was there before, or if it was born in that minute when he saw you getting roughed up, but it's there now."

I went to the door, and she followed.

"Well, I suppose you've gotten what you came for," she said. "You can go back to your life now. Stop looking for us in the papers, Mr. Hardwood."

I stepped out onto the landing and settled my hat on top of my head.

"One of you is going to end up in the morgue because of your stunt, Mrs. Burgess. Now, perhaps it's my morbid curiosity, or perhaps it's my hope that I'm wrong, but I'm going to keep looking for mention of one of you there. Listen, that part of your husband that loses control. You now have to decide if you're going to ever let that monster inside him loose again, or if you're going to let happy, boring old Denton live his life like he wants to live it. My hope is that you'll let sleeping dogs lie, but my money is on you finding another way to push his buttons."

She looked down then, finally feeling shame. "I suppose you're right," she whispered.

"Then I'm going to keep looking for you in the papers, Mrs. Burgess. And when the day finally comes, I'm going to find whichever one of you is still standing afterwards, and I'm going to offer my services to help in any way I can."

"Why?"

"I don't know. Damn me, but I don't know. I do know one thing, though. If you haven't told your husband about you hiring Ed Sparks, you better do so. If not, he may not be at work right now. He might be out hunting your friend down with a tire iron. In fact, you might want to make sure that pistol's still in his underwear drawer. And don't say that isn't who he is because, I think after the other night, all bets are off."

I started down the steps, then. Mrs. Burgess watched me go, saying nothing else, but I hoped -- there it was again -- that she was weighing what I'd said. The smart play would have been to pack her bags and leave. Leaving would take away the temptation to find a way to turn out that animal in her husband's eyes. Go somewhere far away, use her uncle's money and influence to set her up somewhere else so that the day I saw for her marriage didn't come. I'd have driven her to a bus station or the airport, if that was what she wanted. But who could even know? Maybe her running away was the next way to send her husband into one of his newfound rages. And I'd be just enough of a fool to step in between two lovers when they were in the midst of a war.

Out on the street, I looked left, then right. Nothing caught my eye, so I stopped an older fellow tottering along who looked like he might know.

"Say, mac," I said, "there a watering hole around here somewhere? I could use something cold and wet."

"The Old Irish down a ways and across the street," he said, pointing south.

"The Old Irish?"

"Run by a Mexican fella. Go figure." He squinted at me. He had bushy eyebrows, which made it seem all the more profound when he said, "If you don't mind me saying so, it's a little early in the day for that, isn't it?"

"It is," I replied. "If you come along, it could be early in the day for you, too. My treat."

A big smile broke out on his face, and he chuckled. "He keeps his beer especially cold," he said.

"Then let's waste no time. It's hot today already, and it's only going to get hotter before it's done."

Before skipping off with my newfound drinking buddy, I took one last look at the stairs up to the Burgess' apartment. It was noon out, as bright as it could be for the day, and yet the whole of the place seemed thrown into darkness. Long shadows were all around it, which should have been impossible at such a time. But there they were, just the same. And upstairs, I couldn't see into the windows. The curtains weren't drawn, either; there was just no light to see by.

"Odd," I said, and we moved on.